QUANTUM LEAP

OTHER TITLES PUBLISHED BY BOXTREE

QUANTUM LEAP

THE GHOST AND THE GUMSHOE

JULIE ROBITAILLE

BOXTREE

Quantum Leap: The Ghost and the Gumshoe, a novel by Julie Robitaille, based on the Universal television series QUANTUM LEAP, created by Donald P. Bellisario.

First published in Great Britain in 1990 by Corgi Books. Published in 1994 by Boxtree Limited, Broadwall House, 21 Broadwall, London SE1 9PL

1 3 5 7 9 10 8 6 4 2

ISBN: 1 85283 397 1

Cover artwork by Keith Fowles

Printed and bound in Great Britain by Cox & Wyman Ltd., Reading, Berkshire

A CIP catalogue entry for this book is available from the British Library

CHAPTER ONE

My name is Sam Beckett, and I'm a time traveller. I know, it's probably hard for you to believe. That's OK, it's hard for me to believe, too. But it's the truth.

I'm a scientist, a physicist, actually, and I was the guiding force behind Project Quantum Leap, as this time travel experiment is called. Now I'm its chief guinea pig, hurtling around in the space of my own lifetime, entering other people's bodies and identities, solving a few life-glitches as I go. It's all pretty strange, I have to admit.

Perhaps the strangest thing of all is never knowing when it's going to happen, or who I'm going to be . . . or when or where I'm going to wind up . . .

And it was happening again . . .

That off-balance feeling, the rushing and rolling that marked my transition from one time to another subsided and gave way to another feeling, to a sort of calm. It was pitch black all around me as I gradually became conscious again of my body and my surroundings.

Naturally, I had no idea where I was. But my recent experiences with quantum leaping left me with the assurance – although it wasn't a very *comfortable* assurance – that I would soon find out.

Temporarily stumbling and gambling through someone else's life, I would discover whose body I was inhabiting, and what minor little cosmic error I had landed here to rectify. All I knew right now was that the last time I had looked, I had been a minor league baseball player sliding towards home plate, saving the game.

And now . . . well, I thought, peering around, this definitely wasn't any baseball diamond. This was just a thick shroud of inky darkness surrounding me, and there was no crowd cheering me on.

Then I realized that the darkness was pierced by a small beam of light, a beam that emanated from a flashlight I was holding. I looked down, waving it around tentatively, and saw the marble step I was standing on. A marble step in the middle of a black night? Outside? Huh? As I adjusted physically to my new surroundings, I also realized I was shivering – there seemed to be a rising storm wind kicking into high gear.

Somewhere far away, there was the eerie sound of a dog baying at a moonless sky. And I could hear a restless, soft rustling and scratching against something nearby. This was all sort of . . . creepy. I pointed my flashlight in the direction of the sound.

I picked out the shapes of tall, slender poplars, bending low in the wind; their nearly bare branches were being whipped uneasily against a dark marble structure. From where I stood, on the third step down from the blocky building, I could just make out the name 'Claridge' carved in fancy script above a black hole where the door opened into the interior.

Oh, boy, I thought grimly, as the reality of my whereabouts began to dawn on me: a mausoleum. A mausoleum with an open door! Great. Here I am in some mysterious new incarnation, and it turns out to start in a damned graveyard. Great.

The black hole gaped creepily, and I turned away from the sight just as a great, multi-forked branch of lightning slashed and lit the sky. Perfect, I thought grimly, special effects, too. For a brief, brilliant moment, I could see some sort of huge, hilltop manor-like structure, outlined against the sky.

6

Jeeze. If this was how it began, I thought, could Elvira be far behind?

I felt the hackles on the back of my neck begin to rise as the lightning flashed again, and the same dog howled in the distance. Calm down, Sam, I told myself. There's nothing to be worried about. I remembered that when I was very young, my father had taught me never to fear the unknown. He had always impressed upon me the fact that ghosties and ghoulies were dismissable fantasies – nothing more than the creations of an over-active child's imagination.

That *did* calm me down for a moment, until I realized that Dad had probably never found himself in a family graveyard at midnight, unaware of who he was supposed to be, or what he was doing there.

I felt the hackles rise again, and remembered that Dad had *also* always told me to keep an open mind. That wasn't very much comfort, under the circumstances. Then, with a sensation that made my flesh crawl, I knew that there was something behind me. Don't panic, don't panic . . . don't panic! I told myself. I took a deep breath and forced myself to turn calmly around.

I was right, there *was* something there that hadn't been there a moment before. Something – no, some*one* – emerging from the black hole of the mausoleum. A silent, wraithlike creature enveloped in misty white, who seemed to float, rather than walk from the darkness.

I forced myself to stand my ground. I shook my head and blinked, and the figure became more defined. It was a woman – and as she moved a little closer, I could see that she was dark, intense, beautiful, a woman with a cloud of long black hair, whipped into a frenzy by the wind. As she got closer, I could see her blazing dark eyes fixed on some other vision. She could have been real or not. She looked like a Valkyrie. Or a ghost. Or an escapee from a Victorian lunatic asylum.

I swallowed hard. 'Oh, boy,' I whispered.

She seemed to start awake at the sound of my voice. She paused uncertainly on the top step of the mausoleum, her dark eyes now fixed on mine.

'Well?' she demanded. 'Did you hear him?'

'Hear him?' I echoed. It's a technique born of necessity: when you have no idea who or where you are, answering questions by simply repeating them back sometimes makes people impatient or confused enough to just give you the information you need to work with. At the very least, it can buy you a little time.

Her dark eyes were distinctly troubled. 'Julian,' she said. 'You heard him, didn't you? You must have heard him!'

'Julian,' I echoed, nodding. 'Ah . . . no. I don't think I did.'

The woman seemed to sag in disappointment. 'But he kept calling my name!' she exclaimed.

'He did?'

'Tro-ian,' she said, in a sing-song lilt, obviously imitating whatever it was she had heard. 'Troian, Troian!' She stared at me with desperation in her eyes. 'You must have heard it!'

Troian, I thought, what an odd name. I shook my head. 'No,' I said.

'But you must have!' Troian said. '*Please* tell me you heard Julian!' Her intensity was palpable, and I wondered if she really *might* be a madwoman.

Just at that moment, another huge branch of lightning split the horizon. There was a moment of hesitation, of stark silence, and then there was the ominous rumble of thunder nearby.

I seized the moment to make an evasive action; after

all, this conversation was going absolutely nowhere.

'It's going to pour,' I said, indicating the sky. 'Come on, we've got to get to some cover!'

Troian looked at me, her eyes growing large and wild and unfocussed again. She seemed to hover for a moment in indecision, and then she whirled around and disappeared inside the mausoleum again, in a flash of white.

'That wasn't exactly what I had in mind,' I called after her tentatively. The darkness had swallowed her up completely.

But there was no response from inside the tomb, just a thick, heavy silence.

'Great,' I muttered. I squared my shoulders and walked up the steps. Then I entered the mausoleum.

My little flashlight didn't do much to brighten things up as I strolled into the hallway of the Claridge family dead. Everything, I could see in brief flashes, was marble and bronze, heavy with age and portent. It wasn't as horror movie creepy as I had supposed a mausoleum would be – there was no sense of decay or the supernatural, just history and time and . . . well, inevitability. Thinking about death is not one of my favorite pastimes, but it was hard not to in this environment.

I played the beam around the place, and it came to rest finally on Troian. She was far back in the room, and she appeared to be huddled over some sort of marble table. It stood directly below a huge, ornate stained glass window, which, I thought irrelevantly, must be some impressive sight in the daylight.

In a weird way, the entire scene was impressive. One thing I knew about this case already – if you could call what I do 'cases' – there was money here. Old money. Your Average Joe family doesn't have a vault for its dead.

'Dr Mintz!' Troian looked up from the object of her attention. 'Come look.'

I – Dr Mintz, I presumed – wasn't about to rush through a tomb at the dead of night, and hurry into the waiting clutches of a lunatic. Instead, I took my time and looked around me. Checking for hidden booby traps or . . . what? I didn't know.

There certainly were a lot of Claridges who had died in the past century and a half. I let my flashlight beam roam over the drawers that led to their remains. Here was good old Nathaniel Claridge, he bought the farm in 1848. Don't be disrespectful, I told myself – who was I to laugh at the idea of ghosts?

After all, here I was, a time travelling quantum physicist who entered other people's bodies for a living. Accompanied – at least some of the time – by a hologram of . . . Al, who feeds me information about my current assignments on some sort of bizarre need-to-know basis. Al, I thought, where the hell are you? I need to know, I really do.

Just then, the beam came to rest on a handsome bronze bust sitting on a slender wrought iron table. There was a vase of fresh cut flowers on either side of it, giving the whole display an almost shrine-like effect. I peered more closely at the bust.

'Julian Claridge,' the plaque read. '1940-1968.' I studied the bronze face of the young man who had died, a smouldering, Byronic face surrounded by unruly curls. Very romantic, sixties style. A very fitting type for someone who looked like Troian to be crazy about. Literally crazy or not.

'Dr Mintz!' Troian said urgently, 'hurry, please! You've got to see this!'

As I approached her cautiously, Troian grabbed my hand and pulled, convincing me that, despite physical appearances and horror movie surroundings, she really *was* made of flesh and blood.

'Look,' she insisted.

I followed her line of vision and was surprised to see something entirely out of place in this antique setting: an aluminum and glass case, approximately two by three feet in diameter, rested on the marble table under the stained glass window. And inside it was a complicated set up of electronic equipment, with graph paper scrolling through rollers at either end of the machine, and a series of inked needles moving up and down the paper as it worked its way through. It looked like a kind of early electrocardiogram machine, or one for an EEG, perhaps.

I stared at the needles, puzzled. What was a heart or brain machine doing in a mausoleum? For that matter, what was *I* doing in a mausoleum?

I glanced up at Troian and saw that her pale, catlike face was flushed and feverish. She pointed a slender white finger emphatically down at the machine.

'Look,' she said again. 'Look at that!'

I stared, but all I could see was one particular spot where the needles had apparently gone crazy, inscribing a wild series of jagged lines which looked completely out of place.

'See?' she exclaimed. 'I told you!'

I shook my head. 'I'm not sure . . .' I began tentatively. I knew I was supposed to be sure, but I needed more data.

'Oh, Dr Mintz!' Troian said, 'please! It's got to be Julian!'

I scrambled frantically around in my brain for an explanation of what she was talking about. Julian's *what*?

It was as if Troian read my mind. 'It's got to be Julian's voice print, doesn't it?' she pleaded again.

Voice print! What?

'Look at the graph,' she insisted. 'Those lines – they

happened *just* when I told you I could hear him, and what else could explain that?'

Bingo! A light bulb went on in my head as I suddenly put it all together. Julian's voice print. The machine. The dead Julian. The dead Julian's *voice*. This woman believed she was hearing from the dead man. And here I was with her, and she was looking to me for answers. And that meant I . . . well, obviously, I was here to prove or disprove that the dead could talk.

'Oh, Jesus,' I muttered, as the reality of the situation dawned on me in full clarity, 'I'm a ghost-buster!'

'What?' Troian said, puzzled.

'Ah . . . nothing!' I said hastily. 'Nothing at all.'

She bit her lower lip. 'I'm not . . .' she began softly, then stopped.

'Not what, Troian?' I asked gently. Whatever she was, she was scared. And genuine. And she was obviously the one I had been sent here to help. 'Tell me.'

She sighed, a liquid, sad sound. 'Oh, Dr Mintz,' she said, her voice quivering, 'I'm not crazy. I'm not imagining things. I swear . . .'

She was getting distraught again, and I wanted to calm her down – hysteria wasn't going to help me get the information I needed to start *this* loony ball rolling.

'No, of course not,' I said soothingly, 'I know you're not crazy.'

She stared up at me with wide, dark eyes, eyes with depths and secrets and sadness in them. 'Do you?' she breathed. 'Do you, really?'

Well, no, of *course* I didn't really know if she was crazy or not. But she was so blatantly terrified of being just that, that my heart went out to her. And if she was the damsel in distress, I was the white knight. 'Of course,' I assured her, in my calmest tones.

I stared down at the graph paper again, puzzled. I tore

it from the machine, studied it closely for a moment – it still told me nothing – and then carefully rolled it up. 'I'm sure there's something here which will tell us, ah, something,' I said vaguely. 'I'll have to study it, ah . . . later.'

Troian seemed to accept my equivocal statement at face value. That was all very well and good, I told myself, and it bought some time. But there was only so much faking even I could do. I had to get some facts, and I had to get them soon.

Troian sighed and leaned against the cold marble. She cast a wistful gaze at the marble bust of Julian Claridge. Then she turned her dark, somber gaze on me again. 'It's his voice,' she insisted. 'I know it. I heard it.' She stared at me with wide, dark eyes. 'But *how*?' she asked me. 'How can that be?'

She turned away, and I could tell that she was fighting tears.

I put a comforting hand on her shoulder. 'That's what I'm here to find out,' I said.

Just then, there was a searing flash of lightning, visible through the stained glass window. I saw some saint's face light up for a split second, and then the sky went dark again. There was a huge crack of thunder, a clap which penetrated the walls of the mausoleum and seemed to shake them with its ferocity.

This was no night to be out chasing down spooks, I thought. No way, no how.

'Troian,' I began, then realized that she was crying, sobbing softly to herself.

I put my arm around her shoulder. 'Troian, come on. Let's get back to . . .' I thought about the manor on the hilltop and hazarded a guess. '. . . the house?'

She nodded without speaking.

'Some dry clothes,' I said soothingly, 'maybe a little

brandy in some hot milk, I know you'll feel a heck of a lot better.'

I didn't know any such thing. I didn't know exactly where or when I was, and I certainly didn't know how I was going to solve the puzzle of a ghost's voice which came in the night, and had this lovely young woman halfway convinced that she was ready for the rubber room. What I *did* know, however, was no matter who I was supposed to be this time around, no matter who Dr Mintz was, beneath his skin I was still Sam Beckett. And Sam Beckett does *not* spend the night in a family mausoleum with a bunch of dead people and their voices.

'Got an umbrella?' I asked Troian, looking at the sheet of rain which slanted down past the open doorway.

'No,' she said in a small voice.

Of course not, I thought, why inject a note of reality into such a perfectly unreal set-up?

I shrugged. 'I guess we're going to have to run for it,' I said.

CHAPTER TWO

As badly as I wanted to get out of there, I still hesitated at the doorway to the mausoleum. I couldn't remember ever having seen a night quite so forbidding. The rain came lashing down in almost solid sheets, and the lightning and thunder kept up a frighteningly steady crack-and-boom pattern. Still, I thought, resolutely taking Troian's hand, we weren't staying here. Troian with her morbid preoccupation with voices from the dead and her precarious mental state; me with the plain old creeps. We had to go.

'Come on,' I said firmly, and we took off down the slippery marble stairs and into the night ahead of us.

The ground had turned to pure mud, and above us, the tree limbs lashed and whipped up a frenzy, offering no protection against the stinging rain. Troian and I sheltered ourselves as best we could, and slogged our way from the mausoleum steps across what seemed to me like acres and acres of ground.

Finally, we paused, breathless, at the bottom of the rise that led to the looming manor house.

It was some sight: a turreted monster, dark against a darker background. With only a few windows dimly lit, and the sky occasionally highlighted by a fork of lightning, this was right out of Edgar Allan Poe.

I did *not* want to be here – it looked about as welcoming as the mausoleum. But of course, I had no choice.

'You all right?' I said to Troian.

'Yes,' she said weakly.

'Good,' I said, 'it's not much further.'

With Troian clinging to my arm, we made our way up the hill and stumbled up a set of wide steps. I was uncertain whether or not to knock, but Troian solved the problem for me. She pushed the massive oak front door open without ceremony, and we entered.

I could almost hear Troian's teeth chattering in the sudden quiet of the immense entrance hall. It was about the size of a modest aircraft hangar, and lit very dimly by scattered wall sconces made of elaborately curled wrought iron. We stood there, soaked to the bone and dripping, with puddles forming around our feet and gathering on a checkerboard, black and white marble floor. Chess pieces, I thought irrelevantly.

It occurred to me that Troian's already precarious emotional state wouldn't be helped at all by a bout of pneumonia. And who knew what a head cold might do to a time traveller?

'OK,' I said briskly, taking charge of the situation, 'we made it without being struck by lightning. Now, what you need is a hot fire and a hotter toddy.'

Troian shivered and nodded.

'We don't allow fires at Claridge house.'

The chilly voice came unexpectedly from up and behind us, and Troian and I turned, to see a woman standing on the shadowy curved stairway.

'You don't allow fires?' I repeated in disbelief. 'Why not?'

As the owner of the voice made her way down the steps and paused on the closest landing, I got a clearer look at her. I had to stop myself from taking a precautionary step back. Just perfect, I thought, studying her grimly. This is Mrs Danvers' younger sister – shapeless black dress, severely pinned hair and all – come to make this gothic picture complete.

'Why can't we have a fire?' I repeated.

'Oh, it's my fault,' Troian said hastily. She seemed to shrink beside me.

'Yours?'

'I . . . I should have had the chimneys cleaned before I reopened the house . . .'

'Yes,' said the woman in black, staring at me. She had the penetrating glance of a hawk, and her expression was about as friendly. 'You should have.'

'I . . . had so much on my mind, I just didn't think . . .' Troian's voice trailed off.

'Oh, well, you can't remember everything,' I said soothingly. 'After all, how long had it been, again?'

'Three years,' Troian said in a small voice.

Jeeze, I thought, three years?

'Three years is a very long time,' said the woman in black. 'Long enough for birds and . . . other animals to build nests in the chimneys.' Her words were strangely ominous.

Troian shivered.

'A fire would be dangerous,' the woman said. Her tone brooked no rebuttal.

'Miss Stoltz is right,' Troian said meekly.

This was getting ridiculous. I was acting just like Troian, letting this bargain basement Wicked Witch actually spook me!

'So would pneumonia,' I said firmly, staring back at her.

Much to my surprise, this made Miss Stoltz smile, ever so slightly. With a surprisingly fluid grace, she almost glided down the last set of stairs and into the entry hallway. She paused in front of the two of us, staring down at the mud and water at our feet.

'Oh . . .' Troian, said. She bent hastily over and pulled off the flimsy sandals she was wearing. 'I'm sorry . . .'

Miss Stoltz fixed her penetrating glance on me, and I felt as if I was back in the second grade with the nasty ruler-snapping Mrs Beverly hovering over me. I sighed, and pulled off my shoes. I wondered if I was supposed to offer to mop up the hall, as well.

'I'll go and make your drinks,' Miss Stoltz said stiffly. It must have been her concession to our taking our wet shoes off.

Well, a drink was *something*. 'If it's not too much trouble,' I said politely.

Then the gimlet look was back in her dark eyes. 'If you wished to save me trouble, Doctor,' she said, 'you wouldn't be here.'

'Miss Stoltz!' This was too much even for the timid Troian. 'Please try to remember that Dr Mintz is my guest!'

'I'm quite well aware of that,' Miss Stoltz said with stiff resentment in her voice.

Perhaps in response to Miss Stoltz's rudeness, Troian seemed to stiffen, too. 'As long as I'm mistress here,' she said, 'he will be made to feel welcome.'

Not by Miss Stoltz, I thought.

Miss Stoltz stared at Troian with a curious expression for a moment, and then that slight, mysterious smile flickered briefly again. 'As you wish . . . Mistress Claridge,' she said with an odd, uncomfortable formality to her wording.

I half expected her to curtsy, but she simply turned silently from us and glided out of the foyer, then out of sight down some dim hallway that led, I supposed, to the kitchen.

I turned to Troian, whose pale face had taken on a slight flush, perhaps in response to her exchange with Miss Stoltz.

'You'd better get out of those wet clothes,' I told her.

She looked exceptionally fragile, dripping and shivering in her light dress.

'Oh.' Troian gazed down at herself, as if surprised to find her white gown soaked, as if she didn't quite remember she'd just raced through a storm from one kind of mausoleum to another. 'I suppose . . .'

Just at that moment, she was interrupted by another voice from above. 'In case you two aren't familiar with these newfangled modern inventions,' said a young man, 'those things in the closet under the stairs are called umbrellas. People often use them when they go out in the rain.'

'Jimmy!' Troian exclaimed.

'It's me, sis.' The young man winked as he descended the stairs.

It was adding up. Julian's bust, his date of death . . . the three years away from the house. And the way Jimmy looked. I knew approximately when I was, now. I saw the requisite shoulder length hair of the period, the patched, faded bell bottoms, and – surprisingly – a drink in his hand. I would have expected a joint to be there instead.

I was waiting for an introduction, then realized that Jimmy and I – Jimmy and Dr Mintz, the real one, that is – were already acquainted.

'Jimmy,' Troian said eagerly, 'I heard Julian's voice again!'

Jim stared at his sister for a moment, his brown eyes widening in disappointment. 'Oh, Troian,' he sighed. 'Don't start . . .'

'But I *did*!' Troian insisted. 'And Dr Mintz has proof!'

'Listen to me,' Jimmy began, but Troian wouldn't let him finish.

'Show him the papers!' she said to me, and then she

turned abruptly and ran into what I figured must be the living room.

Jimmy looked at me, his pleasant, open face now completely changed; it now registered utter disapproval. 'What'd you do this time, quack?' he murmured.

'Ah . . .' I didn't know how to defend myself. *Was* I a quack?

'Come on, tell me,' he insisted. 'Did you tape the sound track off some porno movie, then play it back at half-speed, something like that?' His tone grew more belligerent. 'Or is it just that you know how to throw your voice? Like some damned ventriloquist – using my sister for his dummy!'

He gave a disgusted snort, then turned on his boot heel and marched into the living room after Troian. I stared after them, exasperated. This was definitely going to be difficult. I had about as much belief in ghost busters and ghosts as Jimmy apparently did, and I couldn't help agreeing that poor Troian shouldn't have her delusions encouraged by some charlatan. But his attitude was obnoxious, and coming on top of Miss Spook Housekeeper and *her* weird approach, I felt my own anger boiling up.

I felt like punching Jimmy in the mouth, or tripping Miss Stoltz with her own broomstick. These didn't seem to be the available options, however. I was here for some reason or other, and the sooner I found out what it was, the sooner I'd be gone again.

'Al,' I muttered.

I sighed and followed the siblings into the living room. It was predictably cavernous and filled with dark, heavy antiques. Weighty red velvet drapes were drawn across massive windows; there was a fireplace big enough to roast an ox in. The walls were hung with tapestries and moody paintings in dark, shadowy colors. Very nice, I thought, just like a movie set. Where, I wondered, is Vincent Price?

Then, across the room, I saw a machine exactly like the one in the mausoleum, sitting on a dark oak desk. Were they everywhere?

Troian came out of an adjoining room with a couple of towels and handed one to me. 'Don't mind Jimmy,' she said softly, 'he's just trying to protect me.'

Jimmy heard her, and moved closer to us. He put his hands on his sister's slender shoulders and forced her to look at him. 'Troian,' he said gently, 'don't apologize for me. I'm doing what I know is best for you.'

'Oh, Jimmy,' sighed Troian. They'd obviously had this quarrel before.

'You have *got* to start getting over Julian's death,' Jimmy told her firmly.

Troian shrugged out of his grasp. 'I *know* Julian is dead, Jimmy,' she said.

'No,' said Jimmy, 'you don't, not really. It's a terrible truth, Troian, but it is the truth – he's dead. He's dead, and he's not coming back, and that's the way it really is!'

'I know that,' Troian insisted stubbornly.

Jimmy threw up his hands in despair. 'Then how can you believe you hear him *talking* to you?'

'Because,' Troian said, her voice low and shaky, 'I hear his voice.'

Jimmy shot me an angry glance. 'How do you know it's not the quack's voice?' he said.

Troian looked up at him, then, her dark eyes flashing as angrily as his, despite the fatigue. 'I'm getting really tired of this, Jimmy. I'm tired of hearing you put Dr Mintz down!'

'Oh, for Christ's sake . . .'

But Troian wouldn't be stopped. 'He's an accredited

parapsychologist, Jimmy, and he's here to try to help me! He's got degrees in . . .'

'. . . voodoo, vampires and zombies!' Jimmy finished for his sister.

I wasn't about to interrupt the shouting siblings. I was too busy drying my face off and studying it in an ornate, gold framed mirror. Hello, Dr Mintz, I said silently to my/his reflection. We certainly are a professorial type.

This still wasn't something I was used to – every time I leaped, I took on the physiognomy of the person whose place I was temporarily taking: it's a very eerie feeling to look into the mirror and see someone you never saw before staring back at you.

'Well?' Jimmy demanded, looking at me. 'What about it, *Doctor*?' The sarcastic inflection on 'doctor' couldn't have been any heavier or more suggestive.

'What about what?'

'Why don't you tell us about what you've seen in your investigations!'

I shrugged. 'I've never seen a vampire,' I said lightly, hoping to defuse the situation. Besides, strictly speaking, it was the truth.

This admission seemed to quiet Jimmy, at least temporarily, and Troian put her hand on her brother's arm. 'Jimmy,' she said softly, trying to make amends, 'I don't want to believe this is happening, either. But I heard Julian's voice, I really did. He called me out to that horrible place.'

'The mausoleum,' Jimmy said, with flat disbelief in his voice.

Troian passed a fatigued hand over her forehead, her resemblance to a gothic heroine pronounced once again. 'I don't know,' she said, her voice almost a whisper, 'Maybe I really am losing my mind.'

Jimmy stared at her with pity and affection, and a look

of utter helplessness. 'Troian,' he said, 'we'll talk about it later, when you're not so wiped out. Go on, honey, go get out of those wet clothes before you catch your death of cold.'

Nice choice of words, I thought.

But Troian didn't seem to notice the implication. 'I *am* cold,' she said with a sigh. 'And exhausted. I think I'll just take a long hot bath, and then I'll try to get some sleep.'

'Good idea,' Jimmy said. 'That's the best therapy, for you, some rest.'

She smiled wanly at him. 'Will you ask Miss Stoltz to bring my hot toddy to my room?'

Jimmy hugged her. 'I'll bring it myself,' he assured her.

'Thanks, Jimmy,' Troian said. Then she looked at me. 'Good night, Dr Mintz.'

'Good night, Troian,' I replied gently. 'Jimmy's right, you should try to forget all about this and just get a good night's sleep.'

'I'll try,' she said. It was obvious from her uneasy tone that a good night's sleep was something she didn't get very often.

I watched her as she drifted from the room on Jimmy's arm, a vague, ethereal creature, beautiful but somehow so distant and wounded that I couldn't even think of her as a real woman, a woman made of flesh and blood.

When they had gone, I turned my attention to the machine on the desk. But no matter how I studied it, it made no more real sense to me than its twin in the mausoleum had. I heard Jimmy come back into the living room, but I didn't look up until he began to speak.

There was barely controlled fury in his voice again. 'Listen to me,' he said sharply.

I looked up at him. His young face was taut and white above tightly compressed lips.

'I'm listening,' I said calmly.

'After Julian died,' he said through clenched teeth, 'I shelled out a lot of bucks, *big* bucks, to *real* doctors, to try to get Troian's head straight again.' He made a gesture with his thumb and forefinger, holding them about an inch apart. 'She came this close to ending up in a rubber room, but she *didn't*! And I'll be damned,' he said menacingly, 'if I'm going to let her wind up in one now, all because of you!'

'I am *not* here to hurt your sister,' I said straightforwardly. 'Quite the opposite.'

'Quite the opposite,' he mimicked me. 'Quite the opposite if the opposite happens to include finding a ghost. Cashing in on it – the lecture circuit, maybe a book. Maybe another "Bridie Murphy," right?'

'No . . .' I began, but Jimmy was on a roll.

'Maybe even a movie, right! I can see it all, now. And if my sister happens to lose her mind in the process, well, so what, right? I mean, why the hell should you care? She's rich. We can just check her into a nice, private sanitorium, right?'

'Jimmy . . .'

He thrust his face up close to mine. 'I'll bet you'd even visit her, wouldn't you . . . once. Maybe twice?'

I couldn't take it any more. I pulled back my arm to slug that insinuating, nasty look off his young face, and stopped only when I heard the dulcet tones of Sister Spook, who had managed to enter the room silently.

'Your hot toddies are ready,' Miss Stoltz announced.

'Fine,' Jimmy exclaimed. He turned and snatched one steaming mug off the ornate silver tray Miss Stoltz carried. 'I'm taking one up to Troian. And I don't want anybody disturbing her for the rest of the night!'

24

He whirled and left the room, and I could hear him stomping up the stairs.

'Is he always such a hothead?' I asked mildly, taking one of the remaining toddies from the tray gratefully. The sweet smell of hot whiskey and lemon and honey greeted my nostrils.

Miss Stoltz fixed me with that look of prey again, her eyes dark, unfathomable.

'Only when he feels his sister's well-being is threatened,' she informed me coolly.

CHAPTER THREE

'I am not here to hurt Troian,' I repeated what I'd told Jimmy to the somber housekeeper. 'I'm here to help her.'

Miss Stoltz sniffed audibly. 'What people say they plan to do and what they really *do* do, often turn out to be two entirely different things, at least, that's what I've found,' she said tartly.

'Well, you must hang around with some really swell, trustworthy folks,' I snapped. Between Miss Stoltz and Jimmy, I could barely keep my temper in check. This entire adventure, so far, had been nothing but discomfort, antagonism, creeps and threats, and I was definitely not enjoying myself.

Miss Stoltz' eyes narrowed down, but she didn't bother to address herself to that last remark. 'By the way,' she said stiffly, 'while you were out . . .' there was clear disapproval of my having been *out*, 'a Mrs Little from the "Lakeview Weekly" called for you.'

Oh-oh, I thought, time to tap dance. 'Ah . . . she did?' I replied.

Miss Stoltz nodded. 'She offered to come up to the house tonight to bring you the clippings you requested from her.'

'Clippings?' I thought quickly. A woman from a local paper, obviously, but what did I want from her? 'Oh, of course! Mrs Little. I asked her to, uh, look up some . . . information for me.'

Miss Stoltz looked at me with a peculiar expression, and I wondered if I was overdoing it. Maybe I should just shut up and stop trying to explain things I couldn't explain.

'So . . . the clippings. Where are they?' I asked.

'I told her not to go to all the bother,' Miss Stoltz told me. 'I said that you'd be happy to drive to town in the morning and pick them up yourself.'

'Of course,' I agreed hastily. 'That was a good idea. There's absolutely no reason for her to come out tonight – as a matter of fact, it could be dangerous.' I gestured towards the heavily draped windows, beyond which lightning and thunder were raging. 'The storm is really getting nasty.'

'It has nothing to do with the storm,' Miss Stoltz informed me coldly.

'No?'

She seemed to stare straight past me, or through me, as if she could see something that I couldn't. 'No,' she said finally. She turned that icy stare on me. 'It's because strangers aren't welcome here.'

Then she turned and slid silently out of the room.

'Gee,' I muttered to myself, 'I'd never have guessed that.' I brought the steaming mug up to my mouth and took a sip.

'You know something, I don't know if I'd drink that, Sam.'

I whirled at the completely unexpected sound of Al's voice, spilling my hot toddy all over a no doubt priceless Oriental rug. My travelling companion was back.

'God damn it, Al!' I said angrily, 'you're doing it again.'

'What?' he said, looking dapper and dry and sly.

'Popping up with no warning!'

'I am,' he agreed.

'I told you I hate that! It's as bad as when you walk

27

through things! And besides, where the hell have you been?' I demanded, promptly reversing myself.

'Well, which is it gonna be, Sam?' Al grinned. 'You want me here, you don't want me here?'

Al, I should tell you, is the hologram projection I mentioned before. He works – or worked – with me on the Quantum Leap time travel project in some capacity or other, although he refuses to be specific about it; he claims another brain behind the project, a hybrid computer named Ziggy, says that I have to get my memory back myself, as much as possible, in order to . . . well, that's another question I don't have an answer to. Although Al *has* hinted that I'm the only one who's going to be able to figure out how to get myself back. To wherever, whenever I came from. I know, it's all very complicated – it even gives *me* headaches when I try to figure it out.

At any rate, Al sort of tags along on these leaps of mine, keeping an eye on me, I suppose, and giving me hints and facts and a little guidance about just what the problem is – what I have to set right, in order to take the next leap.

'I need you here,' I said emphatically. 'By the way, what year is this?'

'1971,' Al replied.

I brightened a little. 'That's what I thought,' I said. 'Good, good – I'm moving forward.' I'd gone from 1956 to 1966, and now, to 1971. Maybe I'd be home, wherever that was, soon. 'Well,' I said briskly, 'let's get moving on this.'

'Good idea,' Al agreed.

'OK,' I said. 'First of all, I don't have the slightest idea what is going on in this haunted house! Let alone what I'm supposed to be doing about it.'

'Weird bunch, aren't they?' Al said casually, glancing

at the remains of my toddy. 'Personally, I wouldn't swallow *anything* Lucretia Borgia there whipped up in her kitchen cauldron.'

'What's with her anyway?' I demanded.

Al shrugged. 'I don't know,' he said. 'But she gives me the creeps.'

'No kidding,' I said sarcastically. 'You don't like the three witches from "MacBeth" all wrapped up in one neat package?'

Al took the question at face value. 'Not a bit,' he assured me. 'You know, it's the weirdest thing, I think she can actually see me!'

That's another thing – Al is invisible to everyone except me.

'Oh, come on,' I scoffed. 'You're invisible! You're just imagining things.'

Al looked around him, taking in the entire immense room at a glance – the heavy, brocaded furniture, the dim wall sconces, the velvet curtains, the musty, deathlike feel of the place. He gave a dramatic little shudder. 'Who the hell *wouldn't* imagine things in a spook palace like this?' he demanded.

'Got the jitters, Al?' I said snidely.

'Hah!' he replied. 'Besides, I don't see you being Mr Calm and Collected yourself!'

'I just escaped from a grave,' I snapped.

'Don't exaggerate, Sam,' Al said absently. 'It was just a mausoleum.' His expression suddenly changed altogether, growing fond and dreamy. Uh oh, I thought, I knew that look.

'You know,' he mused, rubbing his chin thoughtfully, 'this place really isn't all *that* bad . . . it kind of reminds me of this abandoned place in my old neighborhood.'

'Don't start . . .'

'I used to take girls there to . . .'

'Al,' I said warningly. That's another thing about Al, he likes to reminisce about his exploits.

'. . . to go bump in the night,' he finished his sentence triumphantly. 'Listen, it was really great, you know how girls get when they're afraid . . .'

I sighed. 'I don't have time for this, Al. I don't want to hear about your amorous adventures as a randy teenager. Just give me the data so I can get to work, OK?'

'OK,' Al replied amiably. He made a slight waving gesture with his hands, and a holographic computer appeared from out of thin air. He tapped out a code on the keyboard, and watched as the information came up in bright green letters.

'You are Doctor Timothy Mintz,' he informed me, reading from the screen. 'You're a parapsychologist from Stanford who's trying to make contact with the other side . . .'

'I already figured out that I'm trying to talk to the dead,' I nodded.

'Parapsychologists call it the other side, Sam,' Al said reprovingly.

'I know, Al,' I said impatiently, 'I saw "Poltergeist" too.'

'It wasn't as good as Poltergeist, I didn't think,' Al said. 'Did you?'

'Give me a break,' I said, wincing. 'No bad jokes, not now.'

'Anyway,' Al continued, scanning the report as it appeared in front of him, 'here's the bad news – you've been trying, but you've never succeeded in making that break-through contact.'

I shrugged, not surprised at all. 'Of course I haven't,' I said. 'That's because there are no such things as ghosts.'

Al glanced around warily. 'Careful what you say, Sam.

According to Ziggy, this is a very strange house.'

'I don't need a computer to tell me that,' I said with a little laugh. 'It's cold and drafty here, but you can't light fires in the fireplaces – now *that's* strange!'

Al looked at me, his expression sober. 'I'm serious, Pal. Listen to this – all the Claridges in that family boneyard you were in have died violent and unnatural deaths.'

'Oh, come on,' I scoffed. '*All* of them? I don't believe that, it's impossible.'

'Believe it,' Al told me. 'I'm giving you Ziggy's data on this . . .'

'Ziggy has been known to be wrong,' I reminded Al.

I was thinking of a little mishap, during my first quantum leap back to 1956, in which I nearly didn't survive my 'task' of breaking a speed barrier in an experimental jet, in order to save the life of the test pilot who had originally flown it and perished. 'Remember the boiling fuel problem?'

'No,' Al shook his head emphatically. 'Ziggy wasn't wrong there – he had been incomplete in his research, but he wasn't wrong.'

'Semantics,' I shot back. 'We happen to be talking about saving a life . . .'

Al stared at me, his usually merry dark eyes now very sober. 'Well, according to Ziggy's odds, Sam, history is repeating itself: that seems to be why you're here this time, too.'

I felt a sudden chill up my spine, a premonition about what he was going to tell me. 'Are you talking about . . . Troian?' I ventured.

Al nodded.

'Oh, jeeze,' I said softly, 'I just knew it. That poor woman, as if she isn't in bad enough shape already . . . '

Al watched as more information flashed across the screen. 'It says here that she is Troian Giovanni Claridge.

She's a gifted artist, and she was a very successful illustrator – mostly gothic novels – up until three years ago.'

'Three years,' I said, remembering Troian's words, 'that's how long it's been since she was here.'

Al nodded. 'That's right. Because that's when her husband, Julian Claridge – he was the gothic romance writer, by the way, she did all of his covers – that's when Julian died.'

'How?' I asked. 'How did he die?'

Al nodded towards the windows. 'Drowned in the lake out there.' He shuddered. 'And get this – his body was never recovered.'

I whistled softly. It was beginning to make sense, of a sort. 'And Troian?'

Al shrugged. 'She never recovered from it, apparently. They were very much in love . . . and she was there when it happened.'

'Ugh,' I shivered myself.

'Yeah,' Al said, nodding, 'and this was their special country place – they had an apartment in New York and a place in Malibu, which is only about a hundred miles from here; but this was some sort of romantic getaway, they came up here to the mountains for creative retreat.'

'Jesus,' I said. 'Some getaway.'

'Sort of a "last retreat",' Al said.

'Please.' I waved off the bad joke. I thought about what Al had said. 'I can see why she's been reluctant to come back here, but I don't understand, what's with the parapsychologist? I mean, this is a lady in a very fragile state, Al. I – I mean, Dr Mintz – could be driving her right over the edge with all this ridiculous mumbo-jumbo.'

'Keep an open mind, this time around, Sam,' Al warned me. 'This isn't necessarily all "mumbo-jumbo."'

This Tim Mintz is on the level – he's as legitimate as they come.'

I snorted. 'And just how legitimate could that be?' I asked. 'I mean, Al, really! Seismographs for recording voices from the dead – oh, excuse me, I mean, from the other side?'

Al shrugged. 'Who knows?' he said.

'Very scientific,' I muttered.

Al grinned. 'What do you know about science, are you getting some of your physicist memory back, this time around?'

And that's *another* thing – I was apparently a brilliant quantum physicist in the time and place I came from, but that particular ability never seems to show up in my various leaping around states of being. Al thinks it's kind of funny. I don't.

'Al,' I said warningly.

'OK, OK,' he held up a placating hand. 'Well, scientific or not, one thing is for certain.'

'What's that?'

'Mintz really wants to help Troian. In fact, I think he's absolutely crazy about her.'

'Really?' I said. I thought about it, and it made perfect sense. 'She really is very beautiful, in a spooky kind of way . . .'

Al nodded. 'Yeah, I just came from Mintz. He's in the waiting room . . .'

The waiting room is what Al calls where those poor hapless people whose place I've temporarily taken have to hang out, trying to figure out what in the hell has happened to them.

'Where does Mintz think he is?' I asked curiously. Those displaced souls never know.

Al shrugged. 'He seems to think he's been captured by aliens.'

33

I laughed. 'That's a good one.'

'But all he can talk about is how worried he is about leaving Troian.'

'Hmmm . . .' I said.

'And,' Al continued, scanning the screen in front of him, 'he's got good reason to worry.'

'Why?' I asked.

'Because,' Al said, his eyes glued to the bright green letters, 'it says here that unless you prevent it, in two days, Troian Claridge is gonna drown in the same lake her husband did three years ago.'

'Oh, Christ,' I said softly, sinking abruptly down on the nearest chair.

'Yeah,' Al agreed.

I reached unthinkingly for the cooling toddy.

'Sam . . .' Al said warningly, and I pulled my hand back as if I'd been stung.

'Just kidding,' Al grinned. Then his expression turned sober again. 'But Sam . . .'

'Uh-huh?' I said.

'The rest of this is no joke.'

'I know,' I sighed. 'Believe me, I know.'

CHAPTER FOUR

We sat there in a depressed silence for a few moments, while I thought about what Al had just told me.

'Al . . .' I began. There were so many questions unanswered here. 'Listen, you've got to tell me exactly how . . .'

'Oh, jeeze!' Al interrupted me with an exclamation. He was staring intently at his watch. 'I gotta get out of here. Pronto!'

'What's wrong?' I asked, worried that there was an imminent danger to Troian, one he'd forgotten to mention to me.

'Oh!' Al shook his head at my worried look. 'Nothing's wrong, pal,' he assured me, 'but I've got a black tie dinner for the institute, and Merry Wilton, you know that luscious blonde, the one who plays the nympho neurologist on "Break of Day?" She's gonna be a guest.' He winked at me. 'And she's apparently got a very scientific bent. Surprise, huh?'

'Oh, Al,' I cut short his rambling with a look of disgust. 'Give me a break, would you? I need to get some more information . . .'

He shrugged. 'Can't oblige, Sam. I've told you everything I can.' He glanced down at his watch again. 'Well,' he said, unable to hide his eagerness, 'sorry to leave you alone in this horror show, but you know, a guy's gotta do . . .'

'. . . what a guy's gotta do,' I finished the sentence along with him.

'Uh huh. Thanks for being so . . . understanding, Sam.' He winked a lascivious little wink, and was gone.

'No problem,' I sighed, and waved him off as he vanished into thin air.

It really *was* all right. And it wasn't that I was so understanding, either. It's just that I knew from my previous leaps that the information Al could give me at any given time was limited to what Ziggy would allow him to reveal. Whatever questions I'd wanted to ask Al were not deemed appropriate, at the moment. I was on my own.

Well, I thought, let's take stock here. I knew where – somewhere in California – and when – 1971 – I was located. That was a start. And I knew why I was here, which was even better. I knew the time frame I had to work in. Now it was up to me to figure out how to prevent Troian from losing her life in the same gruesome manner that her beloved husband had. In two days. Oh, boy.

I sighed. This was no simple task. This house, its residents, the very nature of the problem – it was an enigmatic situation, at best. A mystery. A mystery, I told myself, in a haunted house. Great. Maybe I'd bump into Abbott and Costello and the mummy.

Well, that was just silly. Haunted houses, indeed! I gave myself a mental head shake. I didn't believe in ghosts. Did I? I was pretty sure I didn't, although I didn't remember, one way or another – it was more an instinctive feeling than an intellectual conclusion. So that meant I didn't believe for one minute that Troian could possibly be hearing the voice of her dead husband speaking to her. Did I? I thought about it for a moment. No, I thought. I didn't.

I sighed and pushed myself up out of the deep leather chair I'd been slouched in. Dark, stormy night, creepy mansion and all, it was time for a little hands-on exploration.

I walked out of the huge living room and across the entrance hall. The room directly opposite the living room was a dining room which could have seated thirty comfortably at a banquet table, polished and gleaming in the dim light. Silver candelabras and two massive, dark wood sideboards hinted at past entertainments, but the room had a musty, unused smell to it, and I concluded that it had probably been more than the three years since Julian Claridge's death since the room had been used. Somebody's ancestors glared down at me from tapestried walls, reminding me that I might bump into Miss Stoltz in my nocturnal wanderings.

I shivered slightly. Ah, I thought, brandy. I took a cut crystal glass from a tray on a sideboard and poured myself a stiff shot. At least I could be sure Miss Stoltz hadn't slipped anything into this drink.

Drink in hand, I made a quick survey of the rest of the front part of the downstairs – a library which could hardly be termed cozy; a white tiled kitchen in which a staff of twelve could have worked without bumping into each other; a smaller study done up in chintz, with French doors which led on to the now pitch-black garden – I figured this had been Troian's own domain in happier times. There were back rooms leading off a narrow hallway, and I guessed they led to servant's bedrooms – no place I felt I had to see that very moment.

I made my way back into the living room, and wandered over to study the machine, the duplicate of the one in the mausoleum. It really did resemble nothing so much as a seismograph, and I still couldn't figure out why I – Dr Mintz, that is – had placed these strategically around the property. How was this kind of graph supposed to pick up a ghost's voice? I frowned down at it, watching the needle move in smooth, even strokes across the paper. Either I had had no experience with this sort of thing in my real life, or I'd completely forgotten it. I voted for the former, but self-awareness wasn't going to provide me with the answers I needed.

Who was 'speaking' to Troian? And why? What was Dr Mintz doing, and how the hell was I going to see to it that Troian wouldn't die in two days. Was it going to be suicide? Accident? Murder? I shuddered at the thought. What was I supposed to do, lock her in her room?

Oh, God, I thought, sinking down in a chair, confused. This is too much: Sam Beckett, quantum physicist, becomes Tim Mintz, ghost buster. I was utterly lost. At least, I comforted myself, as I sipped my brandy, I was moving forward in time. Maybe this would be the last leap before I came back to the present – *my* present. Despite the fact that I was helping people in these various time leaps of mine, I knew I'd be profoundly grateful to return to wherever I came from.

My somewhat rambling musings were suddenly interrupted by an exceptionally violent crack of thunder – it sounded as if it was right on top of the house. An enormous boom shattered the atmosphere, and then . . . all the lights went out.

Perfect, I thought gloomily, what else can happen? I waited for a few moments, hoping the power outage was just temporary; but when nothing happened, and the room remained pitch black and dense, I pulled myself out of the chair I was in, and made my way carefully across the living room, using my hands the way a blind man would use a cane. As I bumped my way past chairs and sofas, I remembered Dr Mintz' handy dandy flashlight, and, swearing softly, yanked it out of my pocket.

I pinpointed my path to the archway that led to the

entrance hall, and headed for it. As I reached it, I was startled by a soft sound from the stairs. I swung the beam of the flashlight up and saw Jimmy Giovanni, paused on the landing shielding his eyes with one hand. The other held a candle.

'Could you get that damned thing out of my eyes?' he snapped.

'Sorry,' I said briefly, slanting the beam down towards the checkerboard floor. 'What happened, anyway? Did the storm knock out the power all over the house?'

'No, Mintz,' Jimmy said, his voice dripping with contempt, 'the boogie man did it.' He stomped belligerently down the rest of the stairs.

'I was only trying . . .'

'Damn it!' Jimmy said. 'Not a flashlight in the entire house! Miss Stoltz must think we're living in the nineteenth century!'

'Where's the circuit breaker panel for the house?' I asked. 'Maybe it's just a blown fuse or something.'

'Why doctor,' Jimmy said sarcastically, 'I didn't know you knew about such practical things – or is that one of the ways you create your special "atmosphere" for your very crazy clients?'

I felt that burning desire to belt him coming over me again. Calm down, I told myself. You're here to help, not to make trouble.

'Your sister . . .' I began.

But my sentence was never finished. Just at that moment, there was a blood-curdling scream from somewhere upstairs. Jimmy and I stared at each other frozen, for a fraction of a second.

Then we raced for the stairs, me in the lead, with the flashlight providing a tiny little trail of light. At the top of the stairs I hesitated – I had no idea where I was going. But Jimmy knew exactly. I followed him down a long, dark hallway to a door which was slightly ajar. From inside, the pale light of a candle flickered.

Jimmy stopped abruptly, and in the vague light, I could see the shock on his young face. 'That's Julian's study,' he whispered, almost to himself. Off my puzzled look, he continued, 'This room has been locked since the day Julian died.'

He pushed the door all the way open, and we crowded through it together. Troian was standing, rigid with shock, in the center of the room, which was filled with sheet covered objects and dust laden furniture.

I couldn't see what it was Troian was staring at so intently, so I made my way gently around her. Her eyes were fixed on the one thing in the whole room which wasn't dusty or covered. I heard Jimmy gasp behind me.

I didn't understand. The object of their fixation, their stunned fright, was just a painting. A lovely painting. It was a watercolor in gentle tones, of a man in Romantic era dress, sitting in a rowboat on a lake. Behind him, I could make out the vague beginnings of the Claridge House. None of that seemed particularly threatening, but there was something odd about the painting. I peered more closely: it was dripping with water.

I looked up at the ceiling, but couldn't spot any sort of leak. Then I glanced from Jimmy's startled expression to Troian's tear streaked face.

'What is it?' I asked.

Troian just shook her head mutely, unable to answer me.

'It's Troian's illustration,' Jimmy explained. 'It was going to be the cover for Julian's book, the one he was working on when he . . . when he drowned.'

'Oh,' I said. But I still didn't see . . .

'I thought you destroyed this one, Troian,' Jimmy said gently to his sister.

'I did,' she whispered. She turned her tortured, tear-stained face towards us. 'I did.' The tears began to flow afresh. 'Oh, Jimmy,' she wailed, 'I threw it in the lake. How can it *be* here?' She began to shiver.

Jimmy and I glanced at each other, and came to a silent, tacit agreement. I took Troian's arm gently in my hand. 'Come on, Troian,' I said softly, 'let's go downstairs, and we'll try to figure this out. OK?'

She nodded numbly, and allowed herself to be led like a mannequin down the hallway and the stairs, back into the living room. I got her seated in an overstuffed chair, and gave her the rest of my brandy, which I'd left sitting there when the lights went out. Jimmy placed the candle he'd been carrying on the table beside her, and the wavering light cast an eerie, dim glow that made the perfect atmosphere for a ghost story. If that's what we were going to hear, and I was pretty sure it was.

'What happened, Troian?' I asked.

She seemed to have recovered a little, but she still had a haunted, frightened look on her face. She didn't look as if she could take much more stress.

'Come on, sis,' Jimmy said, 'tell us.'

'I . . . I was trying to sleep,' Troian began in a shaky voice. 'I was so tired, but somehow I couldn't get comfortable, I kept tossing and turning . . . and then . . . it started again.' She stared at both of us, her dark eyes pleading. 'I didn't imagine it, I swear!'

'It's all right,' I said, trying to keep her calm, 'just tell us what happened.'

Troian took a deep breath and seemed to gather herself up. 'I heard Julian's voice,' she said softly. 'He was calling my name.'

'Oh, Troian,' Jimmy groaned.

'Just let her talk,' I told him through clenched teeth. He threw me an angry glance, but shut up.

41

'I was determined to find out exactly where it was coming from this time,' Troian continued. 'I tried the light, but it blew out. It was dark everywhere, and I could hear the thunder close by – I realized the electricity was gone. So I . . . I lit a candle, and I started to get out of bed.' As she talked, her gaze seemed to turn inward, as if she could see or feel something too horrible to recount. She fell quiet, and then she began to shake, and I gestured towards the brandy.

Troian looked at me as if she'd just remembered I was in the room with her. She took a small sip, and sighed, forcing herself to go on. 'When I swung my feet out of bed,' she said, in a trembling voice, 'there was a . . . puddle of water where there hadn't been one before. I didn't know how water could have gotten there, but I thought perhaps the roof had a leak. I was terribly frightened, but then I heard Julian's voice again, and I thought . . . well, I thought he would *help* me, so I just . . . followed the voice.'

'Then what?' I prompted her.

'I walked down the hallway, because the voice seemed to move, it seemed to be coming from Julian's study, but I knew that wasn't really possible, because the study has been locked since . . . since. Anyway, it was terribly confusing – I followed the voice and . . . it was so horrible! There was a trail of water all along the hallway floor, just as if Julian had come out of the lake and . . .'

Suddenly, her shoulders heaved and she buried her face in her hands, sobbing. Jimmy moved quickly over beside her and put a comforting, protective arm around his sister's shaking shoulders.

'It's all right, Troian,' he said softly, as if he was talking to an hysterical child. 'It's all right, now. We can talk about this tomorrow.'

'No!' She glanced up, her dark eyes flashing wildly.

'No, this can't wait! We *have* to talk about it now, while the evidence is still there! If we wait until tomorrow, it will all be gone, it will all be the way it was before, and you'll think I'm crazy!'

She certainly had a point. But I was becoming convinced that even if Troian was hysterical, she wasn't crazy. Unless . . . the sudden thought struck me with an unpleasant bang, unless she was doing this to herself! And that would definitely put her in the butterfly net category. But why?

Troian passed a fragile white hand through her masses of dark hair. 'All right,' she said, 'I'll be all right.' Then, holding herself rigidly upright, as if that was the only way she could control her shaking, she continued. 'The door was open. I was terrified, but I had to go in. I had to see if he was really there.'

'I don't see how that door could have gotten open in the first place,' Jimmy seethed.

I wished he would stop interrupting his sister's narrative, but I didn't want to start a full blown quarrel with him, not now. Not when Troian was so close to the edge, and when she was so deeply affected by what had happened to her.

'Go on, Troian,' I urged her.

Troian looked from Jimmy to me, then back again. 'He wasn't there,' she said simply. 'Julian wasn't there. But on his desk, his typewriter stood uncovered. It was . . . wet. As if someone had just been using it. Someone dripping.' She shuddered. 'And in it, there was a fresh piece of paper. It had a title on it – it said, "A Portrait for Troian," by Julian Claridge.'

She closed her eyes, her face pale and white and ghostlike, as if the telling of the tale had sapped all her strength. With her eyes still closed, she murmured, 'How could that happen? How?'

CHAPTER FIVE

There was no answer I could give to Troian's desperate question. I couldn't explain what was happening to her, and I certainly couldn't take away the pain and the fear that so obviously wracked her. I glanced helplessly up at Jimmy, who appeared devastated by Troian's story. He didn't have any answers, either.

We stared at each other in the wavering candle light, and then, finally, he sighed. 'I'm putting Troian to bed,' he said wearily. All his earlier antagonism about my presence seemed to have been drained out of him.

'Good idea,' I agreed. 'There's nothing more we can do tonight.'

All three of us trooped somberly up the spiral staircase, Jimmy guiding Troian, who seemed to walk without really seeing where she was going. Jimmy paused in front of a dark oak door – thank goodness, because I have no idea how I would have divined the correct room – and bid me goodnight. Troian whispered it, as well, but her mind was elsewhere – somewhere down the hall, I would have bet.

I walked into Dr Mintz' room and set my flashlight with its beam pointing upright on the old washstand that served for a night table. Without much more than a cursory glance around at the high bedstead with its patchwork quilt, and the large, expensive pieces of rustic country oak furniture that stood against the rough hewn walls, I stripped my clothes off and climbed into bed.

What a night, I thought. What a bizarre cast of

characters. What a mess of a puzzle. I pulled the quilt up and began to go over the events of the evening in my mind, but I found it hard to concentrate. I was wiped out. I'd learned during my first leap – the one back into the test pilot's body in 1956 – that no matter how confused I was by my new situation, I seemed to have the knack of being able to go almost instantly to sleep when my body and brain dictated the need.

Oh well, I told myself, yawning and punching a goosedown pillow into an acceptable shape, I'll think about all this tomorrow. After all, I had two days in which to work it all out. Plenty of time, Sam, I told myself sleepily. Plenty of time. Maybe I was over-estimating my abilities, but still, I drifted right off into slumberland, and didn't wake up once during the rest of the night.

I came awake in a morning which was as sunny and placid as any I'd ever seen; bright yellow light streamed through the curtains, lighting the room cheerfully. It was hard to believe that only hours before, thunder and lightning of gothic proportion had been raging around the house. It took me a few seconds to adjust to where I was, but it all came flooding back quickly. Claridge House, I thought, getting out of bed and pulling on Dr Mintz' clothes. Ghosts and Troian, and an assignment to change a little history by seeing to it that she didn't die.

Hah, I told my – his – reflection in a wavy antique mirror above a country highboy, big deal. No problem. Dr Mintz' eyes looked a little worried, though; and deep down, that was really how I felt. I wasn't so sure I could even learn my way around this house in two days, let alone save a life.

Downstairs in the Titanic dining room, a Victorian breakfast spread was steaming in covered silver chafing dishes. Jimmy, at one end of the massive table, was reading a copy of the 'Free Press,' and wolfing down eggs, sausage, tomatoes, rolls and coffee. At the other end of the table, wan and ethereal, but as beautiful as ever, Troian sat with a steaming cup of tea and a half eaten piece of toast in front of her.

'Good morning,' I said cheerfully.

Troian's eyes lit up when she saw me, and I thought about Al's remark that perhaps Tim Mintz' interest in Troian went beyond the professional. Perhaps the feelings ran both ways – even more reason to see to it that she didn't waste her life by following her husband to his watery grave.

'Good morning,' she said softly. Her voice was low, but calm. The ravages of the night before showed only in a look of fatigue.

Jimmy glanced up from his eggs and his paper, nodded cursorily, and looked back down again. As I helped myself to eggs and toast, I wondered if Jimmy's brief cease-fire in hostility had been just that – a short interlude, to be resumed this morning.

'How are you feeling?' I asked Troian.

She attempted a smile. 'Better,' she said.

Jimmy snorted. 'I think we should just pack up and split from this nightmare castle,' he said.

'But Jimmy,' Troian protested, 'I want to find out what's going on. No,' she corrected herself, 'I need to find out. And I'm not leaving until I do.'

Jimmy shrugged, and threw a mocking sideways glance in my direction. 'Is that what the good doctor ordered?' he asked.

'It's what *I* want,' Troian said with surprising firmness.

Jimmy shoved his plate away, then pushed himself back from the table. His eyes darted back and forth between Troian and myself. 'Then I guess I'll leave you to your exorcism,' he said.

As he stalked out of the dining room, Troian looked at me apologetically. 'He really does want to help, in his own way,' she said.

I had a feeling it was a conversation she and Mintz, the real Mintz, had had before.

'Troian,' I said gently, 'I know that. But what I'm here to do . . .' whatever that was, '. . . is different than what Jimmy can do. I don't take offense at his behavior, I've got more important things on my mind.'

She lowered her eyes, and I saw the sweep of long, dark lashes against pale cheeks. 'I know,' she said softly. She turned her look on me, a dark, intense stare, filled with some sort of promise. 'About last night . . .'

I held up a hand to stop her, I didn't want her rehashing that upsetting experience right now. 'Not now,' I said. 'This morning, I think we should . . .' and I stopped, at a loss. I had no idea what the real Dr Mintz had already done.

'The lake,' Troian said quietly.

'Huh?'

'That's what you said we should do,' she said, a slightly puzzled look crossing her face. 'Look at the lake where . . . it . . . happened. Don't you remember?'

'Of course,' I said heartily. Whew.

We finished our breakfasts – well, I finished mine; Troian picked half-heartedly at her toast, then pushed it aside.

'Shall we go?' she asked. I could sense the tension building up inside her, a reluctance to look at the place where her beloved husband had perished.

'Give me a little while to check on the machines,' I said.

But I spent the next few hours exploring the house,

looking for hidden passages, microphones, any indication that someone was perpetrating a terrible hoax on this woman. My research turned up nothing.

Outside, the sun was brilliant, and birds were singing. The long grass, still wet from the storm the previous night, sparkled and shone with rain drops. We walked silently down the hill past an unkempt rose garden, to where the woods began. Then, after a hundred yards or so, the shaded woodland gave way to a placid lake.

Troian seemed to shudder slightly, but when I turned to look at her, she shook her head.

'I'm fine,' she insisted. 'Really.'

I admired her resolve, but I knew it must be taking a toll on her, looking at that cold, dark water. We walked out on to an old dock, with a faded little rowboat tied to the end of it.

Troian stared hard at the boat. Finally, she spoke. 'We were here,' she began softly. 'I was on the dock, with my painting supplies. Julian . . .' she paused, a catch in her voice. Then she forced herself to continue. 'Julian was out on the lake in that rowboat.' She pointed a slender white hand. 'He . . . wasn't a very patient person, but he was usually good for a half hour of posing before he had to move around. I was doing the illustration for a book cover, his new novel.' She looked suddenly embarrassed. 'Of course, you know that.'

'Just go on, Troian,' I urged her.

'All right.' Her voice sank to a quiet, reflective murmur. 'I don't know what it was, but that day, he was bored – after ten minutes, he was up and down in the boat. He wouldn't stay still – he was clowning around, and then . . . then he was gone.'

'Gone?'

'Over the side. He'd fallen in,' Troian was making a valiant effort to keep her voice from cracking. 'At first

. . . at first, I wasn't worried. Julian was a superb swimmer. So when he didn't surface, I just thought he was playing a game, trying to frighten me.' She closed her eyes, as if to ward off the vivid picture the memory brought forth, then opened them again. 'By the time I realized there was really something wrong, it was . . . too late.'

'You didn't go in after him?' I asked gently.

She turned beseeching dark eyes towards me. 'I can't swim. I never learned how. All I could do was . . . scream.' She sighed, and the sigh seemed to shudder through her fragile body. 'I screamed and screamed, until I couldn't make a sound.'

I looked at her sympathetically, and put a gentle hand on her shoulder.

'I never saw him again,' she said simply.

There was a profound silence on the dock for a moment, while we stared into those unfathomable waters.

'But . . . you heard him,' I ventured.

'Yes,' Troian said softly.

'When was the first time? Tell me again.' I figured the real Dr Mintz had probably already asked these questions, but I was counting on the fact that Troian would trust him/me, no matter what we said.

'The first time was the night they gave up – the night they stopped searching for him . . . his body.'

'And have you ever heard Julian anywhere else, any place but at Claridge House?'

'No,' Troian admitted.

'Have you ever seen him?' I probed.

She shook her head. 'No.'

'Do you want to see him?' I asked.

Troian looked at me, startled. 'Of course I want to,' she replied.

'Why?' I asked her bluntly.

She seemed puzzled by the question. 'Why . . . to talk to him,' she said finally, as if it were the most natural thing in the world. 'To tell him how much I love him. How much I miss him.'

'Maybe,' I said as gently as possible, 'you want to tell him how angry you are at him?'

'What are you talking about?' Troian said defensively. 'Why would I be angry at Julian?'

'For drowning,' I said forthrightly. 'For leaving you behind.'

I suppose it was psychobabble, but then again, it made sense. You loved someone, you got angry if they cut out on you. Even if it was their death that did it. The human mind doesn't always work along rational, logical paths. Sometimes, it just goes on pure, raw emotion. And Troian Claridge struck me as a woman who was emotional in the extreme.

Something I said had struck a nerve. Troian looked at me coldly. 'You're telling me that Julian is dead, and my reaction is that I'm angry?'

I nodded. 'It's possible,' I said.

'Just how selfish do you think I am?' she said tightly.

I shrugged. 'Just enough to be human, Troian. That's all.'

She looked away from me and stared out on to the lake, then at the rowboat, which bobbed gently at the dock. After a few moments, she seemed to put together what I was trying to say.

'Is it . . . do you think it's that I miss him so much, that I'm imagining hearing him?' she asked tentatively.

'It's possible, Troian,' I said softly. 'Isn't it?'

Her eyes were dark pools themselves. 'No,' she said finally. 'It's not. I heard his voice, I know I did. And he sent the painting to me.'

'Why?' I said. 'Why would Julian do all that? Why

50

would he try to hurt you, upset you?'

She took a few steps forward on the dock, staring down into the boat, as if she expected to see Julian appear there, just as he had been three years before.

'Because,' she said in a voice so soft it was barely audible, 'I broke my promise to him.'

'What promise?'

'I promised we'd grow old together,' she said. 'I promised my love would protect him, even here, at the family house. That he wouldn't die, not like the rest of the Claridges.'

It was an awesome burden, an unrealistic burden for a human to carry; I could see why she was so on edge. It was a situation which had tragedy built into it, implicit in its unrealistic promise.

'Troian,' I said firmly, 'you can't do this to yourself any more. We're not responsible for promises that are beyond our power to keep. No matter how sincerely they were made. And you can't *keep* promises like those.'

She looked back at me, and a ghost of something like a smile seemed to cross her face. 'No?' she said.

'No,' I replied. 'You can't stop somebody from dying unexpectedly, Troian. You're not God.'

She turned her head away, a solitary, beautiful figure framed against a pastoral backdrop. She gazed down at the black water. 'I just can't stand the thought of it,' she whispered. 'The thought of Julian down there . . . alone. In the cold. In the dark . . .'

I saw her sway, and realized she was right at the edge of the dock. I leapt forward and grabbed her, just as it seemed she was going to plunge right off the edge and sink into the black waters below. I held her tightly in my arms, felt her trembling.

'It's OK, Troian, it's OK,' I reassured her, although I wasn't at all certain that anything about this was OK at all. 'Take a deep breath. Good, that's good. Now, take another.'

She felt as fragile as a wounded bird in my arms, and I wondered if her grasp on reality was what it should be. Had that been a purposeful sway, a subconscious attempt to join Julian in death? Or had it been an accident?

'Better now?' I asked.

Troian nodded. 'Yes,' she said. 'I . . . I'm sorry. I just got dizzy.'

Maybe. 'It's my fault,' I said apologetically. 'I've been terribly insensitive.'

Troian looked up at me, and once again, I could see that slight flash of affection for Dr Mintz. If only we could get her past the danger, maybe she had a chance at a new life, a happy one.

'I know that you're just trying to help me,' Troian murmured.

We looked at each other intently, and a small spark ignited. Then it was gone, as quickly and fleetingly as it had come.

Troian pulled gently out of my embrace. 'Miss Stoltz will be serving lunch soon,' she said. 'She gets upset if we're late.'

'Jeeze,' I said, 'whose house is it, anyway?'

'Sometimes I wonder,' Troian said thoughtfully.

I glanced up at the house, standing watch over us, and I could have sworn I saw a curtain drop back into place. Someone *was* watching us. But who it was, and what they'd hoped to see was a mystery. Just like everything else here.

CHAPTER SIX

The rest of the day passed uneventfully. Uneventfully, that is, except for the growing anxiety I felt, knowing that the time for Troian's death was approaching . . . and I didn't seem to be able to find any kind of a handle here – a reason for it, *or* a way to prevent it. Troian seemed tired and preoccupied, and I didn't press her any further for facts. I had a feeling that facts weren't going to provide the answers here, anyway.

I observed and snooped all afternoon, but other than the fact that Troian was teetering on the brink, Jimmy Giovanni disliked me, and Miss Stoltz disliked everybody – in other words, things I already knew – there was no one clue that popped out at me. I spent the day feeling frustrated and worried.

Later that night, after an uncomfortable dinner during which Jimmy threw a few requisite snide remarks in my direction about Halloween and broomsticks, Troian excused herself, pleading exhaustion, and went to bed. Jimmy left also, and I was happy to have some time to myself, time without being observed.

I wandered into the living room and began to study the graphs I'd collected from all around the estate. I'd even found one on the dock, which made sense, I suppose, seeing as how Troian claimed that was the first place she'd ever heard Julian's voice. I looked them over again with no results, no ideas.

And then, suddenly, something small clicked. I was finally beginning to make sense of some of the patterns on the graph paper; and as a result, a vague theory about what was going on was beginning to take shape. I couldn't quite put my finger on it, however, and I was just wishing Al would appear so I could test it on him, when I heard his voice.

'Tell you what I think, Pal . . .' he said.

'Hello, Al,' I said, pleased. 'I was wondering where you were.'

'I do have other business to attend to, you know,' he said.

Oh, right. Blonde, brunette or redheaded business, I thought. 'Well, go ahead, tell me, what you think,' I said. As if I could have stopped him.

He materialized in front of me, his expression a little nervous. He glanced around the room, checking to see that we were alone, then peered carefully at the paper I was holding. 'What I think,' he began, 'is that the lake is icy cold, and old Julian just wants somebody down there to cuddle with him, make it a little warmer.'

I almost laughed. 'Jesus, Al . . .'

'You got a better explanation, Sam?' he retorted. He was actually serious! 'You understand what's going on here, in this house of Dracula?'

'Actually,' I replied thoughtfully, 'I think I do.'

'Really? What?'

'I think,' I said carefully, 'someone is working very hard to try to drive Troian insane.'

'Gaslight!' Al said, amazed. He thought about it for a moment. 'Real life Gaslight. I like it, Sam! But . . . who?'

I shrugged. 'I don't know – I mean, I'm not even sure the candidates are limited to this household – who knows what goes on in the rest of Troian's life? That will take a little more investigation. But I have to admit, my first choice is Miss Stoltz.'

Al nodded. 'She certainly fits the part,' he said thoughtfully.

'What's Ziggy got on her?' I asked.

Al materialized the computer out of the air, and glanced quickly at it. 'Hmm,' he said, shaking his head, 'not much at all. She's just a housekeeper. Troian hired her after Julian died to take care of the fun house while she was gone. So she's pretty much got the place to herself most of the time.'

I nodded. 'It would certainly give her the opportunity to bug the place or . . .' and my ideas ran out. 'But there is the problem of motive . . .'

Al seemed stumped, as well. 'Sam,' he said impulsively, 'why don't you just take Troian to Vegas for the weekend?'

I shot him a disgusted look. 'Your mind . . .' I began.

'. . . works quite well, thank you very much!' he shot back. 'I only meant to save her life, for God's sake! Honestly Sam, otherwise, she's gonna drown in that black lagoon tomorrow!'

'I won't let that happen!' I shot back. Then I sighed. 'Listen, Al, it's not a bad suggestion, but think about it. I mean, I suppose I *could* split, and take her with me, but I'm sure it would only postpone the inevitable. If I'm right, someone's out to get her, and a little weekend jaunt to Vegas will only throw a temporary wrench in the plans!'

Al nodded gloomily. 'You're right,' he said.

'What about the brother, Jimmy the hippy?' I asked. 'He's a hostile little son of a bitch – at least, to me. I can't tell if it's protective or defensive hostility. What's Ziggy turned up on him?'

Al flashed another quick look at the computer screen. 'Well, for one thing, he's no hippy – long hair and bell bottoms aside, this is no peace and love freak. He majors in golf and dabbles in investment.'

I whistled. 'No hippy is right.'

'As a matter of fact,' Al said, reading further, 'it looks as if he's got quite a business mind. The investments have paid off.'

'So much for motive, there, too,' I said gloomily.

'Sam,' Al said firmly, 'stop playing private detective and get back on track here. The problem isn't the harpy housekeeper or the snotty little brother. The problem,' he gestured through the curtained window, 'is the Claridge family. The ones in the mausoleum, and the ones in the lake out there!'

'*Ones?*' I echoed in disbelief. 'More than *one* one?'

Al nodded.

'How *many* ones?'

'Ah . . .' Al consulted the computer. 'Three.'

'*Three!* In the lake? Are you *sure*?'

Al nodded. 'Ziggy's sure,' he said. 'This family suffers more drownings per capita than unwanted kittens.'

'Holy . . .' I shook my head. 'Incredible.'

'It all started back in 1840,' Al said, 'when Nathaniel Claridge – that's that nasty looking pirate hanging on the dining room wall – caught his wife Priscilla and the butler in what we delicately refer to as "flagrante delicto" in the attic.' He paused, reading. 'He supposedly drowned them in the lake, and their bodies were never found. Jeeze,' he said seriously, 'that's kind of an extreme reaction, don't you think?'

'Gets you nervous, does it?' I said pointedly.

'Well,' Al shrugged. 'Anyway, they're there. The bodies, that is.'

'They may be there,' I said, 'but it doesn't matter. I don't care *how* many dead Claridges are floating around out there, I don't believe for one second that that really has anything to do with this. They're certainly not who's calling out to Troian, and they're not leaving wet fish tracks to the study!'

Al thought about it for a moment, then nodded. 'I suppose there could be . . . a more natural explanation,' he agreed.

'Thank you,' I sighed. 'Thanks a lot.' I looked at him. 'So . . . what's the more natural explanation? The one I came up with? Someone is trying to drive her over the edge?'

'Well . . .' Al said hesitantly, 'it could be that. Or it could be . . . that Troian is gaslighting herself!'

I puzzled over that one for a moment. 'It's possible,' I said finally. 'But why?'

'I don't know – it was just a thought.' Al shrugged. 'My money is still on Julian.'

'So much for reality,' I said, shaking my head. 'But listen, Al, I've been looking over this stuff – it's planted all around the estate. You know, Dr Mintz' ghost hunting equipment is pretty sophisticated for 1971.' I gestured to the machine in the room. 'It's designed to pick up a wide spectrum of electrical activity, including brain waves.'

'EEG time, huh?' Al said, peering down at the graph.

'Not just that,' I said. 'It picked up my leap in last night.'

Al blinked in surprise. 'You're kidding, right?'

'No. Here, look at this.'

I pointed down at the graph, to a spot where a violent burst of energy was depicted by the extremely peaked waves. 'That's me arriving.'

Al whistled. 'Amazing,' he said thoughtfully.

'I know.'

'What's this?' Al asked, pointing to another set of scribbled lines. They were the same lines Troian had pointed out to me the night before, claiming they were Julian's voice.

'I'm not sure,' I said. 'Troian says it's Julian. And it *resembles* a voice pattern, all right, but there's something . . . weird about it.'

'Well of course there's something weird about it,' Al said. 'It was made by a ghost!'

'Don't be ridiculous,' I said firmly. 'It was not made by a ghost!'

'How do you know?' Al countered.

I had no idea he was so superstitious. 'Because,' I said patiently, 'there are no such things as ghosts, and you know it.'

'I'm not so sure . . .' Al began. 'There are things in this universe which just can't be explained, you know,' he said seriously.

I gave him a look of pure disgust. 'I know that, Al,' I said. 'One of them is me leaping around in time and inhabiting other people's lives and bodies. That might qualify, right?'

'That's different,' Al said.

'How?' I challenged him.

'There is an explanation for that,' he said firmly. 'You just don't remember it!'

'Oh, for God's sake!' I was losing my patience. 'Can we just get back to the business at hand, so I can continue my inexplicable leaps forward . . .'

'God damn you, Mintz!'

It was Jimmy's voice, and he was clearly angry. Al and I spun around in surprise.

'What's the matter?' I asked.

Jimmy came striding into the room, his hair flying, his expression vitriolic. Tucked under his arm he had a large canvas.

He came right up to me, and I could see that his face was flushed, his pupils pinpointed with anger. 'You . . .'

'What did I do now?' I asked warily.

58

'This!'

With an extravagant flourish, he pulled the canvas out and whipped it around so I could see the painting.

'Jesus!' I exclaimed involuntarily.

The painting was horrible – a swirling, furious mass of flaming reds and oranges, all encircling the central figure in the picture: the grotesque black image of a man trapped beneath water. Imagine Edvard Munch twisted inside a surreal Dali lake, and you'll have a pretty good idea of how it looked.

'Where'd *that* come from?' I asked.

Jimmy gave me a look which would have killed if it were armed. 'Why don't you tell *me*?' he seethed.

'I don't know what you're talking about,' I said.

'I had all these destroyed – Troian wasn't herself when she did them, there was no reason on earth to keep them as reminders of what . . .' He broke off abruptly and stared blackly down at the painting.

'Jeeze, that really gives me the creeps,' Al said.

'Well, you should have thought of that before you started this ghost hunt of yours!' Jimmy looked up.

I was too startled to speak right way. No-one had ever been able to see or hear Al before. No-one but me, that is.

'I don't know and I don't even *care* where or how you got your hands on this,' he said icily, 'but I never, ever want to see another one of these again, and neither does Troian!'

'I don't blame you,' Al remarked.

I shot him a look which said 'shut up,' but it was too late.

Jimmy looked as if he was barely restraining himself from going right for my throat.

'I'm not Troian,' he hissed. 'You can't scare me with your bullshit.' His look was pure contempt. 'Throwing

59

your voice, Jesus! How naive do you think people really are? No wonder your kind is always preying on the easy marks – old people, and people like my sister, people too unhappy to question your vicious little charades!'

'Jimmy . . .' I began, hoping to placate him.

'Don't even *try* to explain!' he shouted. Then he forced himself to quiet down, perhaps remembering that Troian didn't need any more upsets. 'Get this straight, Mintz,' he said coldly, 'I don't believe in ghosts. Never have, never will. And none of your tricks will work, not on me!'

'Whew, see you later!' Al said.

I shot the sensitive little creature a dirty look.

'I just told you . . .' Jimmy's voice was rising again.

I watched in utter fury as Al walked right on through his doorway to the future, and it airlocked behind him with a bang!

'Oh, for God's sake, and now you're trying sound effects!'

'No, I . . .'

'I guess creating last night's little spook show must have been a snap for a man of your . . . talents!' His eyes narrowed down with fury. 'Although even you have to admit you got a little help – I mean, *you* didn't create the thunder and lightning, did you?'

'Jimmy,' I said calmly, 'would you just hold it for a minute. What you're saying is ridiculous. I didn't create anything last night.'

'I don't believe you, you quack,' Jimmy shot back. 'I think . . .'

'I just want to help Troian!' I snapped, interrupting him. 'And I'm not a quack!' At least, I was *pretty* certain I wasn't a quack. That's what Al had said. Big deal, I thought cynically.

'You don't give a damn about Troian,' Jimmy snapped. 'You just want to get more grants for your damned quack research, and you'll do anything to make sure you get them. You need a ghost, Mintz, and you'll do anything to see that you get one. *Anything!* Help Troian? That's a laugh! You'd drive her into the nuthouse if you thought it would help you with your career!'

He took a menacing step towards me. 'Let me tell you something, buddy,' he said, his voice low and threatening, 'I'm not going to sit by and let that happen . . . do you understand?'

I nodded. What could I say to convince him otherwise? His mind was obviously made up.

'Good,' he said. 'Then I've got one piece of advice for you. Pack up your Ouija board and be gone by dawn.'

Then he slammed the hideous painting into my chest, whirled and left the room.

CHAPTER SEVEN

I came awake with a snort, and, for a moment, had absolutely no idea where I was. I stared around a vaguely familiar room, confused; saw dark velvet drapes covering huge arched windows, and through them, the first rays of the early morning sun filtering in. Oh, I thought, Claridge House.

I passed a weary hand over my stubbled chin and felt something slide off my lap. I glanced down, and saw that it was a book. Right, I remembered now. After Jimmy had stormed out of the room, I had picked a book of Julian's off a shelf in the library, then come back to the living room and sat down to read. Apparently, I had fallen asleep there, slouched in a deep leather chair. Some watchdog I made, I thought ruefully.

I yawned again, and picked up the book, glancing quickly at it. I had gotten through just about half of it the night before, and I had been, quite frankly, surprised by how readable it was. I was certain that romantic novels weren't my normal taste in literature, but this one had a unique quality to it, a kind of bitter-sweet tone that ran through the tale of celestial love and deep tragedy.

The thrust of the entire story, the writing itself, had a dark, brooding quality, a quality which fit perfectly with the way the bust of Julian Claridge looked. The story would have been a little *too* dark, in fact, if it hadn't been for Troian's illustrations. They provided the relief that Julian's writing didn't; they were bright and whimsical, full of life, not brooding or depressed at all.

Which, on reflection, made the painting Jimmy had thrust at me last night all the more startling in its intensity and effect. I looked over at it, propped against the legs of a small carved table, and shivered. It was hard to look at it.

It was a mad, dark painting, filled with images of pain and death – it was as far from these lovely illustrations as could be imagined. And it was both sad and terrible to think that Troian's mind, her creative spirit, had undergone such a horrible transformation.

I didn't know what I had hoped to find in the pages of the novel, but I felt I was at a dead end. And the finite amount of time I had to change an inevitable outcome was coming to a close. It felt as if a huge hourglass was hovering in the air in front of me, and I was the only one who could see the grains of sand as they dwindled away to nothing . . . to Troian's death.

I reached out to turn the disturbing painting, a reminder of my failure, away from me, when I heard a dog howl in the distance. It sounded more than mournful; it sounded spooked. Almost as if it was trying to warn me of something, I thought, then shook my head. Don't be so fanciful, I told myself sternly. This isn't the time for imagination – this is the time for action.

I hoisted myself wearily out of the chair, and stretched. Tucking my shirt tail into my pants, I crossed the room. As I passed the little table with the ghost detector on it, I glanced down. The needles were wildly scribing across the graph paper, arcing violently up and down. What the hell could be causing this, I asked myself, completely frustrated. What was I missing? There had to be *something*. Something I wasn't seeing.

I yanked open the drapes and stared moodily into the morning. The bright early sun threw harsh rays into my eyes, and for a moment, I was unable to see anything. I heard the howling dog again; this time, it was joined by a chorus of dogs, all baying crazily. Portents and omens, I told myself. What nonsense!

Then, as I shielded my eyes against the sun, I thought I saw a motion on the lawn. Peering into the light, I could just make out a figure on the grass. My heart leapt into my mouth as the figure came into focus: it was Troian, sheer robes streaming behind her, moving blindly, rapidly, across the lawn. Was that what those needles had meant – voices from the dead again? What had Troian heard? And where was she going in that blind, mad dash?

'Troian!' I shouted, but it was no good. She couldn't hear me.

'Oh, God,' I muttered, as she disappeared down the twisted path. It led to only two places – the family cemetery and . . . the lake.

Cursing myself for not having stood guard outside her bedroom door, I whirled and ran through the living room and hall, and out of the house. But by the time I reached the sloping lawn, she was nowhere to be seen. I hesitated for only a moment, then dashed for the lake.

I crashed my way through the trees, arriving on the dock breathless and panic stricken. There wasn't a trace of her anywhere.

'Troian!' I yelled, my voice echoing across the water. But there was no sound, nothing but the howling of the distant dogs, eerie and repetitive, and my own desperate voice coming back to me. 'Troian!'

I glanced wildly at the water, black and placid, barely rippling in the morning light. The rowboat rocked gently, emptily at the end of the dock. No, I thought, she's not here – there was simply no way she could have gotten to the lake and gone in and under by the time I reached it.

The mausoleum, I thought, and spun around. She had to be there.

I raced for it, my heart beating wildly. Al had said she was going to drown, so if she was at the family grave, she was safe. Wasn't she? I didn't know – the whole thing was so crazy, so inexplicable. All I knew was that I couldn't take any chances with her.

I sprinted through the dark woods which separated the two places, and, as I sped through the gate to the cemetery, I could see that the heavy bronze door to the mausoleum stood open. The dogs, an eerie sound-effect counterpoint, seemed to be louder, or closer.

'Troian!' I yelled again. 'Are you . . .'

And just then, just as I stepped foot on the lowest marble stair, I felt myself jolted violently to one side. I stumbled blindly, thrown completely off balance, wondering fleetingly if someone unseen had attacked me from behind; but I couldn't see or hear anyone.

Then, just as I regained my footing, there was a strange shaking and shifting feeling. I felt the ground rumbling under me, saw the trees heaving and swaying above me. It was as if the whole earth was breaking apart, and for a moment, I was completely bewildered. Could I possibly be quantum leaping? No, I thought, that wasn't possible. I had work to do here . . .

'Oh, my God!' I said aloud, as the truth dawned on me, 'it's an earthquake!'

And it was a big one. The rumbling intensified, building to a frightening roar. Still swaying, I yanked myself up the stairs, yelling for Troian; but before I could reach the entrance to the mausoleum, the force of the quake hit again, throwing me to the other side. I watched helplessly as the heavy bronze door slammed shut, cutting me off from reaching her.

I struggled to the top and grabbed onto the ring that opened the bronze door; I pulled with all my might, but it wouldn't budge. The door had lodged firmly shut. The tomb was shaking and trembling, and six inches from where I stood, a crack opened up in the marble stairs. I knew Troian must be terrified. I could hear the sounds of cracking and falling coming from inside the tomb, and I knew instinctively that there was every chance she could be crushed to death in there. Even if the structure managed to hold together, there were marble crypts, sliding drawers filled with the dead.

Suddenly, I heard her scream, and the terrified, helpless sound made my blood curdle.

'Troian!' I yelled, relieved that she was still alive. 'Can you *hear* me?'

There was no reply. Things seemed to quiet down then, and I hoped the worst of the quake was over. I tried frantically to remember the facts of this quake, the 'big one' of the 70s in Southern California. But all I could conjure up was the mental picture of a freeway overpass broken off and smashed to bits, like a child's erector set. Sylmar, that was it! That was the epicenter of that quake, I thought, but how far were we from Sylmar? I had no idea, but the way this quake felt, it couldn't be far.

'Troian!' I screamed again. 'Are you all right? Can you hear me?'

At first, there was nothing but stillness. Then, finally I heard a faint reply. 'Tim?' Troian's voice was tremulous. 'Is that you?'

I sagged with relief. 'Yes, of course it's me! Are you all right?' I yelled through the bronze barrier which separated us.

'I . . . yes, I think so,' she said.

'Hang on,' I yelled, 'I'm trying to get this thing open . . .'

I put my shoulder to the door and strained against it, strained until I could feel the veins standing out on my neck, the sweat running down it. Nothing. The damned thing wouldn't budge at all.

I backed off, took a few deep breaths, and tried to pump myself up for another huge effort. I tried again. This time, it moved. It was only a fraction of an inch, but now, at least, I knew I could get it opened.

'I'm almost there,' I called out. 'Don't worry – I'm coming.'

It took a few more grunting, sweating shoves, but I finally inched the heavy bronze door in just far enough to slide myself through it and stumble into the burial chamber.

The inside of the mausoleum was in bad shape, full of choking, unsettled dust and fallen rubble. Enough sunlight streamed through the ornate stained glass chapel window – which, miraculously, was unbroken – for me to see that the mausoleum had sustained some serious damage in the quake. The floor had buckled and cracked under the stress, and this shaking of the foundation had apparently set off a chain reaction, flinging crypts from their holding places.

I fought my way through rubble and, to my horror, skeletons which had tumbled from their crypts, to get to the back of the room. I could just make out Troian, lying on the floor, hysterical. It didn't take a brain surgeon to figure out why: as if she wasn't having enough problems with reality and death, she'd been knocked down and partially buried under one of the raggedly clad skeletons.

She shrieked as I approached, and I could see that she was desperately flinging dry bones off her, in an attempt to get free.

'Oh, Tim,' she sobbed as I got near.

'Hang on, Troian,' I said, and knelt beside her, shoving a skull with long blonde hair still attached to it, to one side. It didn't take me more than a minute or two to clear the debris and bones off her enough to pull her up to her feet.

'Are you all right?' I demanded, grasping her hand in mine.

'I . . . I think so,' she replied shakily.

'Does anything hurt? Is anything broken?'

'No . . . I don't know,' she said, allowing me to pull her to her feet.

But Troian swayed against me as she said it, and I had to half support, half carry, her, through the gruesome rubble and out the door into the sunlight.

It was all peace and brightness and calm outside the mausoleum. If it hadn't been for the cracked steps and the precarious tilt of the marble building, I could have believed I had imagined the entire quake.

I got Troian down the stairs quickly, in case more damage was to come. As we got clear of the cemetery gates, she started to shake badly.

'Troian, it's OK . . .' I began. 'It's over now, and we've just got to get back to the house . . .'

She looked up at me, and interrupted, her eyes wild with fear. 'They tried to kill me!'

I realized abruptly then that she had no idea what had just occurred. 'Troian,' I told her, 'listen to me. It was an *earthquake*!'

She stared at me, bewildered. 'An . . . earthquake,' she said finally. 'Are you sure?'

I nodded. 'Oh, yeah,' I said, 'I'm sure. And it was a big one,' I added.

'Oh,' Troian tried to digest the information.

'Are you OK?' I asked.

She looked up at me a little more calmly. 'I think so,' she said. 'Although,' she admitted, wincing, 'my leg does hurt a little.'

'Come on,' I said, easing her down to the ground, 'let me take a look.'

She sat on the leaves, and I prodded and pushed, while Troian continued, 'I guess it was pure panic that got me this far.'

'Nothing's broken,' I reassured her.

'I . . . I thought someone was trying to kill me,' she repeated softly, looking almost embarrassed at the admission.

I smiled reassuringly at her. 'You and everyone else,' I said. 'It was an earthquake, and they do kill. But Troian,' I said seriously, 'an earthquake is a terrifying *natural* phenomenon. And they're not at all selective about who they hurt.'

She nodded wearily. 'I know,' she said softly. 'I know.'

'Come on,' I said, helping her to her feet again. 'It's pretty badly bruised, but that's all. How does it feel?'

She tested it gingerly. 'It's OK,' she said, 'just a bit stiff.'

'Here, lean on me. Can you make it up to the house this way?' I asked, putting a supporting arm around her shoulders.

'Yes,' she said more resolutely, 'I'm sure I can.' She limped a little, but managed to move at a good pace. I couldn't blame her – she wanted to get away from that mausoleum as fast as she could, and even a bruised leg wasn't going to slow her down.

'I . . . I want to thank you, Dr Mintz,' she said finally.

'Do I have to play Indiana Jones again just to get you to call me by my first name?' I joked.

'What?' Troian looked at me blankly.

I realized that Indiana Jones hadn't put in an appearance in 1971. 'Ah . . . you called me "Tim" when you were trapped back there,' I said.

'I did?' She looked genuinely surprised, but pleased, as well.

'Uh-huh.'

She looked down at the ground shyly. 'I'm sorry, Dr Mintz,' she said softly. 'I suppose I was a bit panicked when I did that. I know that it's presumptuous to address anyone by their given name unless, of course, they're married. Or related by blood.'

'Are you serious?' I asked, aghast.

Troian looked up at me with limpid dark eyes. 'No,' she said, with a straight face.

We both burst out laughing, and I caught a brief glimpse of another Troian, a normal Troian, ready to laugh and flirt and love. The Troian I'd like to restore to herself. Maybe to Tim Mintz, as well.

'It's nice to hear you laugh,' I told her. 'I like it when you do that.'

Troian nodded, biting her lip. 'So do I, Tim,' she said thoughtfully. 'So do I.'

CHAPTER EIGHT

Claridge House proved to be a solidly constructed building – so solid, in fact, that I was surprised at the comparative damage the mausoleum had sustained.

Inside the house, the powerful quake had caused a real mess – books and vases had tumbled off shelves and scattered and broken; cabinets had been flung open, their contents spilled on the floor; pictures now hung crookedly on the walls, and lamps lay on their sides.

But despite the appearance of disaster, the problems the earthquake had caused here were strictly superficial. They could be cleaned up quickly and cosmetically. Unless there was a structural damage report forthcoming, and I was fairly sure an inspector wouldn't find anything wrong with the foundation, the manor house was really in remarkably good shape. It was quite a relief, and Troian seemed to feel it, too.

An hour after the jolt had rumbled through the Southland, and we had surveyed the damage, the household, such as we were, gathered in the living room to begin the clean-up there. Troian, with her bum leg, was pretty much out of commission, although she did hobble around picking things up until Jimmy told her to please just sit down and stop getting in the way.

Mainly, it was left to me and Jimmy and Miss Stoltz to pick up, straighten up, and hope that a big aftershock didn't come heaving down the San Andreas fault and start the process all over again.

I was quite surprised to see an old black and white

television in the living room. I hadn't noticed it before, and as old as it was, it still looked more than a little incongruous in that stuffy Victorian setting. The picture coming from it was fuzzy and distorted, very difficult to see at all; but the voice broadcast was clear, and Jimmy tinkered with it while we worked at putting the living room back to normal. We watched and listened to the first quake reports being broadcast from Los Angeles. The worst damage had apparently been sustained by a new building, a hospital located in Sylmar, which sat almost directly on top of the fault.

Troian shivered as she saw and heard the early reports about a possible fifty casualties in that collapse. 'Oh, God,' she said softly, 'those poor people.'

I glanced at her and saw a powerful expression of empathy on her sensitive face. The pictures, I realized, must have made her relive her own terrifying experience in the mausoleum.

'It would be like being buried alive,' she said.

Uh-huh, she certainly *was* re-living it, and that wasn't such a good sign.

'Troian,' I said, in an attempt to divert a downward spiral into panic, 'what do you want me to do with this thing?'

I held up a large, cracked Oriental vase for her to see.

'Can it be glued back together?' she asked dubiously.

'I think so,' I said. 'I'll see what I can do with some crazy . . .' and my words trailed off.

I couldn't remember if Crazy Glue had been around in '71. This could be like Indiana Jones all over again . . . but Troian didn't seem to notice the gaffe.

'You know,' Jimmy said from behind the television, 'I can't tell if the quake damaged this antiquated boob tube, or if it's been on the fritz for awhile.'

Troian shrugged.

Jimmy peered around from the back of the television. 'Stoltzie?' he said.

'Yes?' she replied primly. I got the distinct feeling that 'Stoltzie' wasn't her preferred method of address, but she wouldn't give Jimmy the satisfaction of seeing that she disliked it.

For his part, Jimmy probably just got a kick out of tormenting her. 'The television,' he repeated. 'Was it always like this – or did this start after the shake, rattle and roll?'

Miss Stoltz stared blankly at the television, then just as blankly at Jimmy. 'I'm sure I wouldn't know,' she said. 'I don't watch . . . television.'

Right, I thought, you watch . . . astral projections. Crystal balls. Bat wings.

I don't know if Troian was reading my mind, or if Miss Stoltz's stilted phrasing simply struck her as comically as it did me, but she giggled giddily. It was a delightful sound, and I fought back the urge to join her, just in order to keep the peace with 'Stoltzie.'

'What do you watch, Miss Stoltz?' I asked, playing the straight man.

'Not television,' she replied enigmatically.

Ah hah! I thought. I was right! But I went along with the scenario. 'Come on,' I urged her. ''Fess up. You're secretly addicted to . . . "The Twilight Zone," right?'

Well, it was a logical choice.

Miss Stoltz sniffed and looked down her long, pointed nose at me. She wasn't about to dignify that guess with a reply. She turned her odd, intense gaze on Troian. 'If you no longer need me here, Mistress Claridge,' she said, 'I think I should go red up the kitchen.'

'Oh . . . that's fine, Miss Stoltz,' Troian assured her. I could see her fighting the urge to giggle again.

Miss Stoltz swept out of the room in a silent huff. Once

73

she was out of earshot, Troian and I burst out laughing.

'What was that?' I asked.

'What?' said Troian through her laughter.

'Red up the kitchen?' I repeated. 'What kind of language is that?'

'Oh . . .' Troian looked thoughtful. 'I'm used to it, I guess. I don't even notice it any more. It's a Pennsylvania Dutch expression. I think she's, oh, I'm not sure, Mennonite or Amish, one of those.'

'With the buggies and no electricity?' I said, 'You're kidding! How on earth did you find her?'

'Right after Julian died, I ran an ad in the Lakeview Weekly for a caretaker,' Troian said. 'I wanted someone who wouldn't mind staying here by herself while I was gone – I knew I couldn't live here, not for awhile, anyway.' She sighed.

'You just hired her on the spot? I mean, did she have any references or anything?'

Troian smiled ruefully. 'I didn't have much of a choice – she was the only one who answered. And she certainly seemed *qualified*. She said she'd worked here when she was a girl, and she definitely knew her way around, so . . .' Troian shrugged. 'It was a relief to find someone, anyone who would agree to stay in the house by herself. I guess a lot of people think it's kind of . . . creepy.'

'Well, she certainly goes with *that* territory,' I remarked.

Troian smiled. 'Oh, she's not so bad. Not once you get used to her rather, shall we say, melodramatic way of speaking.'

'Oh, right,' Jimmy interjected sarcastically. 'That, and after you get used to the fact that she turns into a bat at midnight.'

'Jimmy!' Troian said reprovingly. 'She might hear you!'

74

Jimmy shrugged and pointed to a spot on the back of the television monitor. 'Here's the problem,' he said. 'The socket for the horizontal hold tube is cracked.'

'Can you fix it?' I asked.

'No problem,' he replied casually, working as he talked. 'A little chewing gum, a little aluminum foil, and . . .'

Suddenly the picture miraculously straightened out and was now perfectly clear.

'. . . bingo!' Jimmy said.

'Wow,' I said, staring at the crumpled pile of debris that had been Olive View Hospital.

Troian apparently thought I was talking about the repair job. 'Oh, Jimmy's a real genius when it comes to anything electronic,' she said proudly. 'He always has been.'

'That's me, all right,' Jimmy said sarcastically, 'a real genius.'

'Well, you are,' she said, looking at him fondly. 'You know what you should do? You should design something that would predict earthquakes! That would be great.'

Jimmy's attention was fixed on the pictures of devastation being broadcast on the television. 'Right,' he said offhandedly, 'I'll get right to work on that, sis. In between the Lakeside Country Club championship and the Crosby Pro-Am.'

Something he said struck a chord in me. I paused in the act of replacing some books which had fallen, on a shelf behind the desk. 'You know what?' I said. 'I think that without planning it, we may have already discovered a rudimentary earthquake detector.' I looked down at the graph.

'What do you mean?' Troian asked curiously.

'You know how the dogs have been howling?'

Troian nodded.

'I believe that they sense quakes coming.' I indicated

the machine with a nod of my own. 'And this equipment may have sensed it, too.'

'But . . .' Troian frowned, 'I was only kidding when I said that to Jimmy. I mean, that's not really possible, is it?'

I put the last book I was holding back in its place, and pointed to the wildly arced graph lines. 'These lines could represent shifts in electro-magnetic energy that precede earthquakes,' I said. 'And the timing is right.'

Troian's expression tightened suddenly. 'Are you trying to say that these aren't Julian's voice prints?' she asked tensely.

'I'm a scientist . . .' I began.

Jimmy snorted in derision. 'Right,' he muttered. 'And Miss Stoltz is Miss America.'

I ignored the dig. '. . . and I'm just trying to keep my mind open to any and all possibilities here,' I finished firmly.

Troian had risen from the chair she was sitting in. I could see that she was upset. 'And the painting?' she demanded.

'What about it?' I replied, bewildered.

'Exactly!' she said. 'What about it? What's your scientific explanation for *that*?'

I stared at her for a moment. 'Why are you so upset?' I asked finally.

Troian glanced at Jimmy, who had ducked back behind the television again, and was fiddling with some other controls. She seemed to want to keep this argument from him, because she lowered her voice to an angry whisper.

'I'm upset because I heard Julian's voice – I know I heard it!'

'And that's why we're here investigating what you've . . .' I began.

Troian cut me off with an angry gesture. 'And if it

76

wasn't real, if these lines represent an earthquake, not his voice, then the explanation we're left with is that I imagined the whole thing . . .'

'Troian,' I started again, hoping to stave off an hysterical reaction, but once again, she wouldn't let me talk until she'd said her piece.

'And if I imagined it, *Doctor* . . .' her emphasis on my formal title, as well as the obvious implication of her sentence, didn't elude me.

'You are not psychotic,' I told her firmly. 'If that's what you're getting at.'

'Not psychotic.' Troian laughed, a sharp, bitter laugh. 'What am I then? Merely mildly hallucinatory?' she said.

'Listen . . .'

'And what does one do about a "merely mildly hallucinatory" patient, Doctor Mintz? Lock her away for a little while? For good?' Her dark, sad eyes demanded an answer.

'No-one said anything about locking you away, Troian,' I told her. 'That's not the issue.'

'Maybe not for you!' she shot the words at me. 'But it's one of mine. *Believe* me, it's one of mine!'

'The issue is finding out exactly what is causing this reaction.' I pointed to the graph again.

'Why must you keep looking for other explanations, then?' Troian exploded. 'I thought you wanted to prove that Julian's spirit is haunting this house as much as I did!'

I couldn't tell her I didn't believe in ghosts; at least, Tim Mintz, psychic phenomena investigator, couldn't tell her that. 'I want the truth,' I said calmly. 'And I believe you do too.'

'The truth is that Julian won't let go!' Troian cried desperately.

I reached out to touch her, but she shrugged my hand away.

'And the truth is,' she said, looking sadly at me, 'I'm not sure I want him too.'

Limping a little, she pushed past me and headed out of the room. She paused briefly in the doorway and glanced back. She took a deep breath, tried to calm herself. 'I'm going upstairs,' she said in a shaky voice. 'I'll see you both at lunch.'

'Not me . . .' Jimmy began, but Troian was already gone.

'Where are you going to be?' I asked curiously.

Jimmy didn't look up from the TV. He pointed at the picture. 'I'm going to L.A. I wanna see this mess in person.'

I looked at him in disbelief. 'You're kidding, right?'

'No. Why?' He asked without much curiosity.

'Because it's a disaster area!' I said. 'The last thing they need is gawkers!'

Jimmy shrugged. Then he snapped off the television. 'Too bad,' he said. 'I think it should be really interesting . . .'

'You callous little . . .' I let the words trail off. What good would they do?

As he headed for the door, he gave me a smile that was closer to a sneer than a friendly grin. 'What's the matter, doc? Getting nervous?'

'Why would I be getting nervous?' I asked him pointedly.

Jimmy shrugged. 'Sis didn't seem to be too happy with you just now,' he said maliciously.

'She's upset,' I said firmly.

Jimmy snickered. 'Troian's got more on the ball than you think,' he said. 'Maybe she's finally catching on to you. Maybe you're about to be . . . cut off.'

Once again, Jimmy Giovanni had pushed me too far, and I reached out and grabbed his arm, prepared to shake some sense or manners into him.

Jimmy stared down at my hand on his arm and then up at me. He shook his head and pulled his arm from my grasp.

'Don't blow it, man,' he said with a nasty wink. 'Don't wanna blow your source . . .'

And he was gone, leaving just an unpleasant aftershock behind.

CHAPTER NINE

I took a deep breath and forced myself to calm down. Temper wasn't going to help me find the answers to this riddle any faster. I thought about it, and decided to take advantage of Jimmy's departure and Troian's self-imposed exile in her room – where she was, for the time being, safe – to snoop around. I was beginning to have certain suspicions about this set-up, and I thought I had a good idea where to look to confirm them.

I retrieved a small tool kit from my room, thanking the absent Dr Mintz for his forethought, and left the house again. It was time to take a closer look at the inside of the mausoleum. Although it was tough to get myself to walk voluntarily back into that place, it had to be done.

The destruction was mind-boggling, even more apparent, now that the dust had settled and I had time to look around. Almost all of the wall crypts had been wrenched open by the force of the earthquake, and their grisly contents were spilled all over the floor, lit by the sun which streamed incongruously cheerfully in through the broken roof.

The walls hadn't been strong either, it appeared, because some of the floor crypts had also collapsed, leaving gaping holes in the structure. The rear wall had partially caved in, as well; and I could see the earth and tree roots through the gaps.

I shivered. There was no doubt that this was a very dangerous place to be; the entire structure looked as if it were in imminent danger of total collapse. And I certainly had no desire to join the legions of Claridge dead, resting happily in bits and bones on the floor.

I picked my way very carefully around the open crypts, trying not to shake or move anything as I went. At the back of the room, I located the ghost detector. I marveled that it, like the stained glass window, was still intact – the most fragile things in the place had survived the quake, in one of nature's little cosmic jokes.

Better and better, I thought, as I studied the machine: it was not only intact, it was still working.

As I set my tool kit down and began to rummage through it, I heard a pneumatic hiss, as if a door was opening. I knew without looking that Al was making an appearance.

'Psst!'

I looked up to see him peeking around the corner of his door to the other place.

I bit back a grin – he looked so nervous. 'What is it?' I asked. 'Are you coming all the way in?'

'Is anyone here with you?' Al asked.

'Nobody that will hear you,' I replied.

'Good.' Al sounded a little more relaxed.

His whole body appeared in the chamber, and the door wheezed shut behind him. 'Yikes!' he jumped a foot as he noticed our bony companions. 'Jesus, Sam! Why didn't you warn me?'

I watched with amusement as he whirled and tried to get back through the door. It was no longer visible, and he fumbled clumsily with his ever-present computer, in an attempt to make it reappear. 'Come on, come on . . .' he muttered.

'Hey,' I said, 'calm down. Just wait a minute before you go anywhere, OK?'

'But there are dead people in here!' His usually cynical, bright eyes were darting around the crypt nervously.

'Al, stop whining! I've never seen such ridiculous behavior in my life!' I chastized him.

'Oh, really?' he snapped, affronted.

'Yes, really,' I replied. 'Do you realize how scary you'd be if someone else could see you walking through walls that don't exist?'

'There's nothing in the least scary about a hologram,' Al said snippily. 'That's a scientifically explainable phenomenon!'

'Uh huh,' I replied, turning back to my explorations.

'How do you explain a ghost?' he demanded.

'There are no such things as ghosts,' I replied patiently.

'Oh, yeah?'

'And I can't believe we're actually having this conversation,' I continued, ignoring his disbelief.

'How can you sit there and say there are no such things as ghosts,' Al demanded, 'in the middle of all this?' He gestured theatrically around the mausoleum.

I sighed. 'Those are skeletons, not ghosts.'

'Well, I think I saw one of them move!' Al declared.

I didn't even bother to look up. I busied myself removing the access plate to the ghost detector. I began to examine the circuits carefully.

'I need your help, Al,' I told him. 'This equipment of Dr Mintz's is even more sophisticated than I thought.'

'Tell me about it,' Al said gloomily. 'Somehow or other, that damned thing is actually allowing people to hear *me*!'

'I know,' I said, concentrating on the wires and connections. 'If that idiot Jimmy had half a brain, he'd realize that no-one is that good a ventriloquist.'

Al shrugged. 'He seems a little more intent on . . . other things in life.'

'Yeah, well . . .' I squinted at the wires. 'Do you think

this is picking you up through my brain waves or direct?'
I asked.

'I don't know, and I don't care,' Al said firmly. 'All I
know is that I very definitely don't want people other
than you hearing me.' He paused reflectively. 'Not
unless,' he added, 'they're women.'

'You mean like that blonde?' I asked, pointing over his
shoulder.

He fell for it. 'What blonde?' he asked, turning.

From the open crypt behind him, a female skeleton
with long blonde hair still attached grinned maliciously
at him.

Al gave a shudder and turned away. 'That's not funny,
Sam,' he said. 'I'm not into necrophilia!'

'Hallulujah!' I said, working away.

'You find something?'

'I just meant, hallelujah, at last I've discovered something sexual that you aren't into!'

Al looked affronted.

'How can I alter this circuit to pick up low voltage
battery emissions?' I asked, turning the conversation
serious again.

Al peered over my shoulder. 'Well,' he said, 'you can
start by disconnecting that hot pink wire – that one, over
to the left.'

'Hot pink?' I said, amazed.

'Hot pink,' Al assured me, pointing. 'It was a very in
color back in the early seventies,' he reminisced. 'Day-
glow, all that stuff. Gee, remember micro-mini skirts?'
His voice was wistful.

'I sure do,' I said, just as wistfully. Then I shook my
head. 'Come on,' I reminded him, 'we've got a job to do
here.'

'I know, I know,' Al told me. 'Let me take a look at
that thing.'

Al, of course, couldn't touch anything – holograms have that little problem. But he could point and show me precisely where to poke and prod, how to connect, reconnect, disconnect the right wires and terminals. I just followed his directions.

'OK,' he said after a few minutes, 'give it a try now.'

I turned on the power, and one of the needles promptly began to scratch across the graph paper.

'It's working,' I said, a little amazed.

'Of course it's working!' Al sounded peeved. 'Now walk around with it, see what happens.'

I did as I was told, watching the oscillations of the needle vary as I moved. 'I think it's picking up a battery. Somewhere in the tomb.'

'Uh-huh,' Al said, 'keep going.'

Eyeing the movements on the graph, I walked straight over to one of the few unbroken ground crypts in the place. 'I think this is it, Al.' I pointed to the crypt.

Al grimaced as he read the inscription. 'This one's pretty . . . fresh,' he observed.

I followed his gaze. 'Fresh?' I echoed in disbelief. '1948?'

'I don't know, Sam,' Al said, backing away, 'it might still have some . . . yucky stuff.'

I figured this was as good a time as any to pay no attention to him. I plunged ahead, pulling the lid back from the crypt. It slid off rather easily.

'Hey, Al,' I said, peering into the coffin, 'check this out.'

Al kept his hands over his eyes. 'Do I have to?' he said.

'Come on!' I said impatiently.

He dropped his hands and peered in alongside me. 'Oh ho!' he said, forgetting his revulsion.

Beside the skeleton, still dressed in almost intact clothes, lay a tape recorder.

'Oh ho is right,' I said, reaching in and pulling it out. I laid it on top of the sarcophagus. 'Here's our ghost,' I said.

'Come on,' Al urged me.

I switched it on, but to my surprise, there was no sound, no voice, nothing at all.

'This is a very quiet ghost, Sam,' Al observed.

'All I can hear is tape hiss,' I agreed, frustrated.

'Thank God for discs,' Al observed.

I stood there, frowning and puzzled, when suddenly, a dog began to howl. I looked instinctively over at the ghost detector, and sure enough, the needle that had inscribed the strange voice prints was moving again.

'Al,' I said, 'look at that.'

But there was no voice coming from the tape. So how could Troian be hearing voices? It just didn't make sense. Unless . . .

'Al . . .' I hazarded, talking my thoughts out, 'is it possible, I mean, could you record a voice to only be heard by ears which are ultra-sensitive to high frequencies?'

Al looked bemused. 'Like dogs?' he said. 'I suppose so.' He nodded. 'Yes, I'm sure you can.'

'Dogs,' I repeated, 'and some people, too. I've read about it – they're usually *women!*'

'Sam, are you trying to say that Troian has this . . . ability? To hear at high frequencies?'

'It makes sense,' I said excitedly, gathering steam as my theory took on a definite shape. 'Think about it!'

Al frowned. 'It does make sense,' he admitted, 'but it would be really tricky. I mean, it would take a genius at electronics to pull it off.'

I stared at him. 'That's right,' I said. 'A real genius. And I know that one of those just happens to live at Claridge House.' I stared at the recorder. 'That bastard!' I exploded.

There was our villain, and here was his method. But there was no time to waste thinking about the whys and hows of Jimmy Giovanni's schemes. 'Thank God Jimmy is gone for the time being,' I said grimly. 'We have a chance to get Troian out of here before . . .'

'Sam!' Al exclaimed, his voice filled with sudden dread. 'Listen – there may be no time at all!' He pointed to the recorder. 'This thing is remote controlled and gang-loaded.'

'He could be controlling it from anywhere . . .' I realized.

'Not just this one, Sam,' Al said grimly. 'If there are other recorders hidden around the place . . .'

'Like in Troian's room,' I said, all of it becoming clear now.

Al nodded. '. . . that's right. And if there are, you may have just turned them on, too.'

Which meant that Troian, even as we spoke, could be hearing voices, the voices that had already sent her close to the edge. This might be the one to push her over . . .

'Oh, Jesus!' I said, spinning around. 'I've got to find her!'

'I'll find out where she is,' Al called after me.

As I raced through the door, hoping I would be in time, I could hear Al behind me.

'Gushie,' he was saying to someone from the other side, 'have Ziggy center me on Troian, now! And I don't want to hear about any over-loaded circuits. This is a matter of life and death, and it's coming down now!'

CHAPTER TEN

I fled from that mausoleum as if a pack of wild dogs was chasing me. Hoping against hope that Troian hadn't heard anything yet, hoping against hope that even if she had, she hadn't acted on its commands yet, I sprinted through the woods and up to the house as fast as I could. By the time I reached the manor, my heart was pounding with a combination of the exertion and just plain fear.

'Troian!' I screamed.

I burst through the heavy front door and looked wildly around. Standing at the bottom of the spiral staircase, I shouted for Troian, hoping that she'd hear me no matter where in the house she was. If she *was* still in the house.

'Troian!' I yelled. 'Troian, are you here?'

Nothing greeted me, nothing but an ominous silence. I started up the stairs, taking them three at a time, shouting her name all the way.

'Troian!' I paused briefly at the top of the stairs. 'Troian, answer me!'

First, I thought, her room. I raced to it and flung the door open. No trace of Troian. Julian's study, I thought, and whirled around. I burst into the dark, shuttered room, but it, too, was devoid of all life. Suddenly, I noticed the painting of Troian's, that nightmare effort of hers. It seemed different, somehow, and I peered at it more closely.

'My god,' I whispered, horrified.

The painting had been altered since the night before. And now, instead of the one black figure, Julian, trapped in the lake, there were two. And the second figure was, quite clearly, meant to be Troian, with her long dark hair swirling around her in the water . . .

This was it, I thought, this would be the sign, the portent, that would send Troian right over the edge. She would see this, and she would believe it was time to join Julian in death.

I had to get to her. I spun around just in time to see the door slam shut. I hurled myself against it, but it was no use. I tried again and again, but the heavy door was locked, and I was trapped. Locked in. Unable to reach Troian or to save her from what must inevitably be her death.

'No!' I shouted. Then, 'Al! If you can hear me, for God's sake, *do* something!'

I gazed frantically around and headed for the shutters. They were nailed shut, but not very effectively. I pounded and ripped and finally tore them free. Then I yanked the window open.

The drop from there to the ground was sheer, and although I didn't think it would kill me, I couldn't take a chance that anything might hobble me. I climbed precariously out on to the narrow ledge that ran the length of the building.

I looked to my right and my left, gauging my escape route. I thought I might just make it to a nearby drainpipe, and shinny down. I looked down and shuddered. Don't do that, I told myself. Don't look down.

I edged my way shakily across the ledge, and reached for the drainpipe. My foot suddenly shot off the ledge and for a moment, I was sure I was going to tumble headlong to the ground below. But I was just able to hoist myself back up and get a firm grasp on the drainpipe. Then I began my descent. The moment I hit the ground, I was off, running.

I knew exactly where Troian was, and I knew where Jimmy was, too. He hadn't gone to Los Angeles to survey earthquake damage – he was right here, wreaking some damage of his own. But I wasn't, I told myself as I raced across the grounds, going to let him get away with it. Not a chance.

I burst through the trees to the top of the sloping lawn, and suddenly I could see them!

I could just make out their two figures on the dock – Jimmy and Troian, locked in some sort of embrace. I shouted, but I was too far away to be heard. I could see that Jimmy had her by the arms, and she was struggling to get away. Then, I saw her knock him aside with a surprising burst of strength.

I was too far away to do anything but yell. As I watched helplessly, Troian tried to run towards land, but her bruised leg put her at a disadvantage. Jimmy took after her and was gaining, when suddenly the earth rolled and shook. It was an aftershock, a big one, and I'd never been so glad to feel anything in my life.

That galvanized me into action again. I dashed for the lake, my heart pumping furiously. As I raced those last few, long yards, I saw Jimmy catch up to Troian once again. She'd been knocked off balance by the force of the tremor, and Jimmy was taking full advantage of the situation.

I watched, horrified and helpless as he grabbed her and dragged her by the arm to the edge of the dock. They struggled there.

'Troian!' I screamed. 'Jimmy!'

I saw him glance wildly at me, then at the lake. Something seemed to spook him – maybe just the realization that there was a witness. He took a small hesitant step backwards.

Even from that distance, I could see the madness in

his eyes. He turned, and with a mighty shove, he pushed his sister over the edge and into the water. She disappeared with a shriek.

'You son of a bitch!' I screamed as I flew up the dock. I tackled him, shoving my shoulder into his gut. The force of the attack tumbled us both over the side of the dock and into the lake.

I gasped as I hit the cold water, then popped up again. I had to get to Troian, Troian who *couldn't swim*. I took a deep breath and dove. The water was dark and cold, and there was no trace of her.

I popped up again and took another breath.

Just then, Al appeared at the end of the dock, tapping madly on his computer.

'Ten feet to the left of where you are and eight feet down!' he shouted.

I nodded, turned and dove. There was nothing, nothing but darkness . . . and then I saw her, limp and floating, as if she was one of the family ghosts already.

No, I thought, no! I churned furiously through the water and grabbed her, kicking us both to the surface of the lake.

'Troian!' I sputtered. 'Oh, God, you've got to be alive!'

I looked down at her pale face and then she shook suddenly. She coughed, gasped for air, and her eyes popped open. 'Oh, Tim,' she said, gasping.

A pang of relief swept over me as I stroked toward the shore, pulling her with me. I helped her up on to the dock and looked around for some sign of Jimmy. There was nothing, not a trace.

But with a shiver, I realized that there were three other bodies floating on the surface of the lake.

'Jesus,' I whispered. 'What happened?'

Pale, dripping, shivering, Troian shook her head. 'It

was Jimmy,' she said, her eyes huge and dark with shock. 'It was Jimmy all along!'

'I know,' I said gently. 'If only I'd figured it out sooner . . .'

She shook her head. 'How could my own brother . . .' she let the words trail off. Then she looked up at me, and I could see the pain and the sorrow there.

'He . . . he told me that he had just planned to drive me mad,' she said in a heartbroken whisper. 'He had a . . . drug habit . . . and he owed a lot of money to some people in Vegas.'

'So it was all about money,' I said.

Ziggy, I thought, you screwed up again.

Troian nodded somberly. 'He thought, with me put away, he'd be able to get control of all the money . . . Julian's money.'

'I already know how he did the voices,' I told her. 'But the painting?'

Troian shrugged. 'He did those, too. Jimmy has . . . all sorts of talents.' Her voice was tinged with bitterness and resignation.

I didn't know if this was worse than a ghost, this betrayal by someone in whom she'd trusted completely. But at least she was alive.

*   *   *

Some time later, we were wrapped in blankets and dealing with a half dozen people who had come in response to my urgent phone call. The three bodies I'd seen floating in the lake were now neatly laid out on the dock.

Troian shivered beside me. 'I don't think I can stand this, Tim.'

'Yes,' I said, 'you can.'

'My own brother,' she said. 'What he tried to do . . .

I would have given him anything he asked for, if he'd just asked.'

'He is . . . was . . . a very sick person, Troian,' I said softly. 'It's not any kind of excuse, but that's what you have to remember.'

'I can't do it,' she said.

'Yes, you can,' I repeated firmly. 'You got through Julian's death, you got through all the horrors Jimmy put you through . . .'

'I guess he didn't think it would be so difficult to drive me mad,' she mused. Then she looked up at me, and despite the anguish, I could see that there was a spark of new hope in her eyes. Of the will to fight.

'What is it, Troian?' I asked gently.

'When we were fighting on the dock, I told him that I wouldn't die for Julian, and I damned well wasn't going to die for him!'

'You're a survivor, Troian, despite everything.' I looked seriously into her eyes. 'That's the difference between you and Jimmy.'

Troian nodded grimly, as the coroner joined us. 'I'm afraid there's no sign of your brother, Mrs Claridge,' he told her. 'I'm sorry.'

'Yes,' Troian said, gazing enigmatically out across the lake.

'Drowned trying to save you, did he?'

Troian stared at the dark water, seeming to consider the question. Finally, she turned her gaze on the coroner. 'Yes,' she said. 'That's exactly what happened.'

'Ah . . . who are the bodies?'

'It's the most amazing thing,' said the coroner, shaking his head.

Mrs Little, from the local paper, joined us. 'I think,' she said, 'you'll find that this is Nathaniel Claridge's wife and his butler. He drowned them nearly a century and a half ago.'

'Good God!' I exclaimed.

'And the third?' Troian asked softly.

The coroner nodded sadly. 'I believe it's your husband, ma'am,' he said, confirming her thoughts.

'But . . . a century? Three years ago? How could the bodies . . .' I was utterly bewildered.

The coroner shrugged. 'This lake is deep,' he said. 'Temperature at the bottom is probably close to freezing.'

'So they were just . . . preserved?' I said, amazed.

He nodded. 'They look better than some of the fresh dead I've seen . . . no disrespect, Mrs Claridge.'

'But . . . why now? Why would they surface now?' I asked.

The coroner shrugged. 'The quake must have shaken them free of whatever held them down there,' he said. He turned to Troian. 'Mrs Claridge, I'm sorry, but I'm going to have to ask you to identify your husband.' He saw her look of panic. 'Take your time,' he told her, and walked away.

Troian turned to me. 'I'm scared,' she said.

'I know,' I nodded, 'but I'm here.'

She looked a little startled, as if she had just realized something. 'Yes, Tim, you are,' she said softly. 'You've been here for me the whole time, haven't you?'

'Come on,' I said gently, 'you can handle it.'

Troian took a deep breath and nodded.

We walked to the end of the dock, where the bodies lay, draped with tarps. The coroner looked up at Troian and lifted one.

We stared down at the handsome, perfectly preserved face of Julian Claridge. Then Troian dropped to one knee. 'Julian,' she whispered, touching him softly on his cold cheek.

93

I left her with him to say her goodbyes, and stepped back. Mrs Little came up beside me, gazing at the strange tableau at the end of the dock.

'I guess you won't be needing those clippings, now, will you?' she asked.

'Clip . . . oh!' I remembered suddenly what she was talking about. 'No,' I said, 'I won't.'

'You know,' Mrs Little volunteered, 'this is actually more exciting than finding a ghost – murder victims recovered after one hundred and thirty years – who would have believed it?'

'It is rather astounding,' I agreed.

'After this, I doubt there's much that anyone could tell me that would surprise me.'

I bit back a smile, wondering what she'd say if I told her who I really was . . .

'Oh,' I said casually, 'I don't know.'

Troian approached us, pale but composed. She took my arm and addressed the coroner and Mrs Little. 'If you'd like to come up to the house with us,' she said graciously, 'I'll have Miss Stoltz put on some hot coffee and tea.' She glanced around. 'I think we could all use it.'

And that's when I knew that Troian Giovanni Claridge was going to be just fine. That she could finally put the horrors of the past behind her, and get on with her life.

'Did you say . . . Stoltz?' Mrs Little enquired curiously.

'Yes,' Troian replied. 'Do you know her?'

'No.' Mrs Little shook her head. 'But it's quite a coincidence . . .'

'What?' Troian asked.

'Well, Nathaniel's wife Priscilla was a Stoltz,' Mrs Little said. 'Mennonite, I believe. At least, from Pennsylvania.'

'How odd!' Troian said. 'Maybe she's related. We'll have to ask her.' She smiled up at me.

I felt a little twinge of cold apprehension race through me.

'Ah . . . why don't you go ahead,' I said, gently disengaging her arm from mine. 'I'll be right along.'

'What?' Troian said. She glanced from me to the shrouded bodies at the end of the dock. I saw a look of intuitive understanding cross her face. 'Oh no you don't,' she said. 'We're in this together, Tim. After all, it's your work.'

She stayed resolutely by me as I walked back to the end of the dock, and motioned the coroner to pull the tarps off the other two bodies, the ones from the nineteenth century.

The man was young and handsome, but I wasn't interested in him. My gaze – and Troian's gaze – moved quickly to the woman's body that lay beside him.

Troian gasped. 'It's . . .'

And it was. It was Miss Stoltz. And she had the faintest smile on her face.

'What's wrong, Dr Mintz?' Mrs Little asked me. 'You look like you've actually seen your ghost.'

And I had. I closed my eyes. Come on down, Tim Mintz, I thought. There are a couple of ladies waiting for you . . .

And everything went black.

CHAPTER ELEVEN

I suppose I should have been getting used to these transitions; but I found that each time I leaped, it was still more than just a bit of a shock to my system – it was a kind of complete disorientation. There was always that overwhelming sensation of rushing, rolling darkness – that feeling of being off balance, almost out of body, until I landed wherever I was going.

I wasn't precisely sure what was happening to me physically in this time travel of mine, and Al refused to enlighten me. I had to figure it out (or remember it) for myself, he claimed. So far, I didn't. But anyway, there was the initial swept away sensation, and then, with an abrupt thump, I emerged into another time, another place, someone else's body. And with that new body, someone else's problems.

One thing stayed with me during this particular leap: I was eager to test my forward-motion theory. As I became aware of my surroundings, I wanted to find out the facts immediately – would I be closer to my own actual 'real' time?

Maybe . . . I would actually be there, where I came from. A respected quantum physicist again, memory intact. I couldn't wait to find out . . .

The darkness and haze whirled away, leaving me standing alone in another strange new location. It appeared to be a dim moonlit office, and something about it struck me as being slightly odd. The lighting, I realized. Or lack thereof. It was all black and white and vertical stripes cast by the moon filtering in through the Venetian blinds. Very film noir, I thought, very . . . moody. But not at all familiar.

Then I looked down, and gasped. 'Oh, Jesus!' I exclaimed.

At my feet lay a person. Dead, I thought immediately, and took an involuntary step backwards. I forced myself to remain calm. Then I looked down again. It was still there, all right.

It appeared to be the body of a gray haired, burly man, face down in a pool of blood. His own blood, no doubt. I peered at his back. Bullet holes, three of them, told the story.

'Oh, Jesus,' I repeated.

Just then, I realized I was holding something in my hand, something heavy. With a shaking feeling of trepidation, I brought my hand up, and in the silver moonlight, I saw the metal glint of the revolver I held.

Oh boy, I thought, this is great. What kind of bizarre situation had I landed myself in this time?

'Al . . .' I began, hoping that sneaky little hologram would appear on demand, like a genie from a brass bottle. But I had no chance to even finish the sentence.

Behind me, the door to the office blasted open noisily, giving way to the impact of two determined bodies – two uniformed cops who barreled through the doorway, their pistols pointed directly at my heart.

I dropped the gun I was holding and put my hands in the air. 'Officers . . .'

'Freeze!' yelled one of them.

I was already frozen, but this hardly seemed to be the time to quibble.

'This isn't what it looks like,' I said. 'He was dead when I got here.' But even as the words came out of my mouth, I realized they sounded feeble, like lines from a bad movie.

One of the cops, a wire-thin man with what looked like a permanently cynical sneer on his pockmarked face knelt to pick up the gun I'd dropped. 'Really?' he asked, lifting one eyebrow cynically.

'That's not the . . . murder weapon,' I said feebly.

'Uh huh.' He used a pencil to pick up the gun and wave it in front of my face. 'Anybody besides you and . . .' he indicated the body with a nodding gesture, '*him* to corroborate that?'

'Ah . . .' I wracked my brain, but, of course, I'd just arrived here – literally – a few moments before. How would *I* know? 'Not . . . well,' I stumbled, trying to find the words to explain. There weren't any, not any he would believe. I shrugged. 'I don't know,' I confessed.

Al, where the hell are you? I thought.

The other cop, a beefy, weary veteran of too many crime scenes, sighed. 'Right,' he said. 'Of course you don't know.' He moved up beside me and cuffed my wrists with great expediency. 'Well, I guess if that's your best answer, Mr Allen, it looks like you can plan on missing the Dodger opener today.'

The Dodgers?

'I'm still in L.A.?' I said, actually to myself, but how could the cops know that?

The wiry cop sneered. 'L.A.?' he said. 'Sure, bud. And Ebbets Field is now in Hollywood.'

He chuckled as his partner pushed me towards the door. 'Don't even bother to try that crazy amnesia bit with us, Allen – it won't wash.'

I took in his words about the Dodgers with growing consternation. Uh-oh, I thought as I glanced quickly around the office, then, finally, down at myself. The battered blond furniture, the upright manual typewriter

. . . my natty, baggy pinstriped suit. No wonder this had the look of film noir, I thought, no wonder it felt black and white. This *was* black and white. Because if the Dodgers were still in Brooklyn, then I was . . . in the fifties! The fifties!

I wanted to scream. I wanted to stamp my feet. Far from moving forward in time, I'd leaped back, and *far* back!

'Al . . .' I muttered. If he'd been there, I would have tried to strangle him. It would have been pointless, he's a hologram. But the urge . . .

'Save it, bud,' the burly cop remarked. 'You can scream for your mouthpiece all you want . . . once we've got you booked.'

Oh, great, I thought, as I allowed myself to be led passively away. Just great. I knew that Al would show up sooner or later, but I just prayed it would be sooner. Like *before* I was tried and convicted of a murder I had no knowledge of. Before I took that long, last walk to the chair . . .

We rode through Manhattan, and I shrugged off thoughts of capital punishment and stared around me with wonder at the fifties – the cars, the clothes, the buildings – that I had only seen in movies before. I stoutly refused to answer any questions the two cops asked, and they seemed glad to turn me over for booking.

Inside my Manhattan precinct cell, I took stock of my situation. Since I had begun quantum leaping, I had become quite adept at quickly picking up information about my whereabouts and who-abouts. By the time I was fingerprinted and mug-shot, then locked unceremoniously in a tiny little cell, I already knew it was April, 1953, and that the Brooklyn Dodgers were playing their season opener at home against the Pirates.

I also, and more importantly, now knew that I was

Nick Allen, a private eye, and that the man who lay dead on the floor of Nick Allen's office was his own – my own – partner. Phil Grimsley.

I sighed. I'd seen some very peculiar looks thrown my way as I was marched through booking, and now, as one of my nearby inmates crooned drunkenly, I walked over to the tiny mirror above the sink in the cell. What did I look like this time?

'Fairy tales can come true. It can happen to you . . .' the drunk warbled in the background. '. . . if you're young at heart . . .'

'Oh my God!' I yelped. The man in the mirror, Nick Allen, looked exactly like . . . Humphrey Bogart! 'Holy . . .' I muttered.

'Play it again, Sam.'

I whirled to see Al grinning at me. 'Al!' I said. 'I don't get it . . . who *am* I? Am I Nick Allen, or am I . . . *him*?'

Al shook his head. 'No. You're not him. He's in Long Island with Bill Holden and Audrey Hepburn, making "Sabrina".'

'But . . .'

Al shrugged. 'Who knows?' he said philosophically. 'Genes, genetic quirks . . . distant relatives, who can tell? Maybe that mug is the reason you – Nick Allen – became a gumshoe in the first place.'

'Gumshoe,' I echoed.

Al threw me a look of disdainful impatience. 'Shamus,' he said. 'Tec. Dick. Don't you dig the lingo?'

I shrugged. 'I . . . I don't remember,' I said. 'But they all mean . . . private eye, right?'

'Great,' said Al, 'your deductive powers are working already – some peeper you're gonna make!'

'Al,' I said, 'it's 1953.'

'That's right,' he replied cheerfully. 'It was a very good year for stockings and garter belts.' His eyes misted over with some fine sexual recollection I didn't want to know about.

'It's 1953,' I repeated. 'How did that happen? I'm supposed to be travelling forward!' I said.

'According to who?' Al said quizzically.

'I . . . I don't know!' I replied, frustrated. 'I can't remember.'

'And that's part of the challenge,' Al said pompously.

I gave up, frustrated. This was going to be another of those go-nowhere conversations with Al. I changed the subject and pointed to the reflection in the mirror, 'Well at least I remember him!' I curled my lip into a facsimile of the famous stiff sneer. 'Here's looking at you, kid,' I said, and winked.

'Are you done playing?' Al asked drily. He materialized his omnipresent computer. 'Because if you are, there is a little business we're supposed to be taking care of.'

'Sorry,' I said, chastened. Having Bogart's face was . . . I don't know, like having a toy or something. 'I'm ready now,' I assured him. 'So, what's the deal – what am I here to do?'

Al gazed at the computer screen. 'Probably . . . to find the killer,' he said nodding. 'Yeah. Well, that makes sense.'

I felt a sudden elation and relief. 'Then I didn't do it. I mean, Nick Allen didn't do it. Right?' I asked hopefully.

Al's gaze was fixed, intent. 'Ziggy says it's four to one against,' he said, wrinkling his brow.

'Ziggy!' I exclaimed in disgust. 'How the hell can I trust Ziggy? He's the one who said Jimmy Giovanni was rich!'

Al shrugged. 'We all make mistakes, Pal.'

'Some of us make less important mistakes!' I exclaimed. 'Ones that aren't life threatening!'

'Do you want to get back to the business at hand?' Al queried mildly.

I nodded.

'OK,' he said. 'Phil, the dead partner, apparently did some shady work – seedy divorce cases . . .'

'Oh, really?' I asked. 'Did you have him on retainer?'

Al quirked one warning eyebrow at me, then returned to his task. 'He was probably offed by someone he lensed in a compromising position . . .'

I waded through the lingo. 'Who?' I demanded.

Al turned to me and shrugged. 'No data available on that,' he said. Then he grinned. 'You're the shamus. You figure it out.'

I sighed. This was ridiculous. 'I'm not a . . . shamus,' I said.

'You are now,' Al said matter of factly.

Right. Like I'd been a test pilot and a ghost buster. And had to bumble my way through those. I stared into the dim little mirror again. Seeing Bogey's face was a sort of inspiration, though, I had to admit that much. What a kick! I mean, you look like Humphrey Bogart, you figure you're going to act like Sam Spade. Right? It must come . . . naturally. The idea grew on me, and I sneered at my reflection cockily.

'You dirty rat,' I muttered, hitching up my pants with a sort of swagger.

Al snorted derisively. 'That's Jimmy Cagney, Sam. Not Bogart!'

'Oh,' I said, chagrined. I suddenly remembered. 'Right.'

'Well, peeper,' Al said cheerfully, 'now that you're all settled in, I've got to be going.'

'Wait a second!' I protested. 'You've got to stay for awhile, help me . . .'

Al shrugged genially. 'Sorry. No can do,' he said. 'Tina's got this friend . . .'

'Give me a break here Al,' I said, pained. 'You've got to hurry away so you can cheat on Tina with one of her own friends?'

Al looked mildly offended. 'Tina's got this friend,' he repeated patiently, 'who knows a guy whose kid works for a trainer who's got a sure thing running in the fourth at Santa Anita today.'

'Oh,' I said.

'Now don't you feel bad for jumping to such sleazy conclusions so quickly?'

'No!' I snapped. 'I'm in jail for a murder I didn't commit in the year I was *born*, for Christ's sake!'

'That's right,' Al agreed.

'I don't know what I'm supposed to do or how I'm even supposed to get out of here, this cell, I mean, and all you're worried about is some nag in the fourth . . . and that's supposed to make me feel *better*?'

'Well . . .' Al said. He made a comme ci-comme ca gesture with his hand, but he didn't look as though the scenario I'd just described bothered him very much.

Suddenly, I had a . . . well, I won't call it a vision. I just had a prescient feeling that swept over me with a palpable rush. 'Al!'

'What?'

'I'm going to get out of here.'

'Well, yeah,' he said, edging away. 'I kind of figured that.'

'No,' I said impatiently, 'I mean, I'm going to be set free. Now.'

Al looked at me as if I was out of my mind. 'Really?' he said. 'By who?'

'You!' The word came from the crocked crooner in the cell across the way.

'Jeeze!' Al jumped. 'Can he hear me, too? Like Jimmy

Giovanni? Maybe something's wrong with my program, I should talk to Ziggy . . .'

Just then the crooner broke into song. 'You, you, you . . .' he sang, 'I'm in love with you.'

Al and I exchanged looks of relief.

'I can't explain it, Al,' I said. I shook my head, bemused. 'But somehow, I know that any second, this big fat detective with a cigar in his mouth is going to come around that corner . . .'

'Give it up, Sam,' Al said wearily.

'. . . and tell me that I'm being set free because they found out that the bullets that killed Grimsley didn't come from my gun!'

'You're cracked,' Al said calmly.

Just at that moment, a heavy set detective rounded the corner. He had a soggy cigar clamped firmly in the corner of his mouth, and he wore a disgruntled expression. Trotting alongside him was the turnkey.

'You're out of here, Nick,' the heavyset man said gruffly.

I turned and smirked at Al, who just shrugged helplessly.

'Detective Lannon says . . .' the turnkey began.

Lannon turned a disapproving eye on him. 'I can talk for myself, sonny,' he said. He turned back to me as the embarrassed turnkey unlocked the door to the cell. 'Ballistics confirms it, Nick,' he said. 'The bullets that killed your partner didn't match your gun.'

'Deja vu!' Al exclaimed.

'No,' I said, 'I don't think so. That can't be right.'

Lannon shot me a very peculiar look – he thought I was talking to him. 'Fine,' he said. 'Stay here for all I care.'

'No!' I said hastily. 'I didn't mean that the way it sounded. Not at all.'

'Then what did you mean?' Lannon eyed me curiously, as if I was a specimen in a jar or something equally fascinating and repugnant.

'I meant . . .' I shrugged, at a loss for a plausible explanation. An explanation that Lannon would find plausible, at any rate. 'Nothing,' I said. 'I just want out. Really.'

Lannon shrugged. 'OK. But listen, Nick. You're still a suspect. So don't go getting any fancy ideas . . . or itchy feet. Got it?'

I slid past the turnkey and into the corridor. 'No problem,' I said cheerfully. I was out!

'If you're out of here,' I heard Al say behind me, 'so am I, Pal!'

I glanced back and saw Al disappearing through the wall, with a little wave and a grin.

'Oh, no!' I said. 'You can't leave now . . .' I grabbed the bars to the cell. 'Al!' I shouted. 'Come back!'

But he was gone without a trace. And I was left on my own, in an unfamiliar Manhattan of years gone by, in the middle of a murder case. In which I was one of the suspects. Possibly, the only suspect. And no matter whose body and whose face I had, *I* knew I was no detective. I didn't have the faintest idea where to begin.

I sighed and turned to see Lannon with the most peculiar expression in his eye. He and the turnkey exchanged knowing glances and shook their heads in grave unison.

'Heh, heh,' I said, shrugging into my overcoat. 'Ah . . . heh, heh!'

Lannon shook his head. 'You know what your problem is, my boy?'

I certainly did, but my real problems weren't exactly what Lannon had in mind. 'No,' I said humbly.

'You've been hit in the head with a sap too many times,' he said, nodding sagely.

I grinned feebly.

'Come on, what are you waiting for?' the turnkey demanded.

'Nothing,' I replied, and followed my captors meekly along the corridor to freedom.

Behind me, the crooner broke into another off-key chorus of 'You, you, you . . .'

Maybe getting away from that incessant noise was the best thing about getting out of jail, I thought morosely. God only knew what waited for me on the outside . . .

CHAPTER TWELVE

Under the stern eye of the Watch Commander, I signed for Nick Allen's confiscated personal belongings – wallet, watch and keys – and then emerged, a free man, on to the mean streets of Manhattan.

Below me was a pavement which could tell a couple of million stories. Above me was a gray, threatening sky. In my dark gabardine trenchcoat and low slung fedora, I felt like I was the walking epitome of private eye-dom. My – Nick's – Bogey's – face creased in a properly cynical smile, and I observed the world through jaundiced eyes, thinking how seldom things looked the way they really were.

Rounded yellow cabs tooted their horns; women walking fluffy little poodles sauntered down the streets, seams in their dark stockings straight and inviting; young news vendors hawked their wares. People rushed by, unseeing, uncaring. It was so perfectly New York, so perfectly fifties. So brisk and above board.

But beneath that bustling exterior, I knew there lurked a different world, a world where crime and evil flourished, a world where teenagers with switchblades terrorized their helpless prey, a world where – even as I walked – people were laughing at the same 'I Love Lucy' episodes they'd still be watching forty years from now . . . No, wait a second, I thought, frowning, that didn't make any sense at all. And besides, where had this unexpected poetic streak sprung from?

I shrugged and hailed a cab. There just wasn't time

enough to stand and ponder life's little mysteries, not when my assignment was to solve a big one.

'Where to, bud?' the cabbie asked as I climbed into the back seat.

'Ah . . .' I fished around in my pocket and pulled out Nick Allen's wallet. He had a small stack of business cards tucked neatly into one corner flap. 'The . . . Gotham Towers,' I said, reading off one of them.

The cabbie eyed me in the rear view mirror. 'Say,' he said. 'Are you . . . '

I smiled my cynical smile and shook my head. 'No,' I said.

'Really? Come on, I won't make a scene or anything,' he said. 'It's excitin' to have a celebrity in my cab . . . somethin' different to tell the guys at the garage. You know, I had Dinah Shore just last week.'

I met his gaze in the mirror and shook my head again. 'Honest,' I shrugged, 'I just look like him. But,' I couldn't resist adding, 'I *am* . . . a private detective.' After all, that was almost as glamorous as being a movie star.

Well, then again, maybe it *wasn't*, because the cabbie's expression went immediately from eager to churlishly bored. 'Big deal,' he said, and that was the last of our conversation.

He screeched to a halt in front of the Gotham, a towering mid-town office building, its stern granite facade relieved by black marble and brass deco designs. A real beauty, I thought, gazing upward through the window of the cab. I paid the driver with Nick's money and thanked him, but he squealed away, eager to get to his next transient connection to the stars . . .

Stop it! I told myself. Stop with the purple prose. I straightened my shoulders, tugged my fedora, and marched into my – Nick's – place of work. Phil Grimsley's place of death.

The lobby was even more impressive than the facade of the building. Richly veined black marble, stainless steel and brass alternated in panels along the walls. The marble floor was buffed and polished. There was a busy concession stand selling candy and magazines in one corner, and a conversation grouping of oxblood leather chairs and couches in another.

The only discordant note in the entire perfect scene was the tinny radio, which was playing someone who sounded exactly like the drunken crooner I'd gratefully left behind in jail. And he was singing that same damned song.

The chorus, 'You, you, you . . .' followed me annoyingly as I strolled towards the elevator, trying to look as if I knew exactly where I was going.

Luckily, I'd made a note of Nick Allen's office number when I'd gotten the address for the cabbie, and I knew that 'Grimsley and Allen, Discreet Investigations' was located on the fourth floor of the Gotham. It wouldn't do for a detective – a tough shamus, a good gumshoe – to be seen staring at the building's directory looking for his own office number.

Suddenly, I paused in mid-stride. I had that overwhelming feeling of deja vu again. It was as if I had been not just in this place, but in this time, in this precise moment, before. As if I was reliving every step towards the elevator.

And I knew with sudden perfect clarity that someone was about to speak to me, someone named . . . Seymour. And that Seymour would have something to do with publishing.

Just at that moment, a hand tapped me tentatively on the shoulder, and I whirled around to see a little old lady staring up at me.

'Seymour?' I said dubiously.

She looked at me blankly, then shook her head. 'Bogie?' she asked hopefully.

I shook my head, too. 'I'm afraid not,' I said politely. 'He's out on Long Island making a new picture with Audrey Hepburn and William Holden,' I added conversationally.

Her expression went from curious to furious, and to my complete surprise, she promptly whacked me with the patent leather purse she was carrying. 'Masher!' she said. 'You shouldn't go around pretending to be him!'

'But I wasn't . . .' I began to protest.

She cut me off with a finger which she shook vehemently under my nose. 'I know what I'm talking about, young man,' she admonished me.

'But . . .'

'And anyway, if you know so much, what's the name of the movie?'

'Sabrina,' I said humbly. 'It's about a chauffeur's daughter and two rich brothers . . .' the words trailed off.

She stared at me suspiciously and sniffed. 'That Audrey girl is too skinny,' she said. Then she turned on her sensible black heel and strode angrily away.

Maybe, in a funny sort of way, Detective Lannon had been right, I thought, bemused. It wasn't that I, Sam Beckett, had been getting hit with a sap; but maybe leaping from one year to another had not only turned my brain into Swiss cheese – something Al occasionally claimed he believed – but had also made my brain a receptacle for paranormal flights of fancy as well. Seymour, indeed. And publishing? What was I picking up in that mind of mine?

I sighed. But then it happened: I heard someone call my name. 'Nick!'

I turned slowly to look at the newsstand, the spot where

the exclamation had come from, and the guys who were grouped around it. And then I knew that my prescience, or whatever it was, was the real thing. Because I knew exactly what I would see there.

I knew the stand with its metallic grille, crammed to overflowing with stacks of newspapers, offering up candy bars and Chiclets and Fan-Tan and coffee. I knew that there were too many different kinds of pulp rags and True Crime kinds of magazines to even fit into any kind of order. And I knew, if I got closer, I'd recognize the names and the covers of those rags.

But most of all, I knew exactly *who* I was looking at. There were two men standing in front of the concession. One, the tall, mild looking one was Lionel; he was the Gotham building superintendent. The other, a shorter, chubby man, was Chuck, and he was the elevator operator. And behind the stand, responsible for the candy and the magazines was . . . Seymour. The one who had called my name.

I checked him out quickly. He looked to be about twenty years old, and as if he might have to take those Charles Atlas ads seriously if he wanted to stop getting sand kicked in his face by big local bullies. He was . . . a kid. A skinny, pimply kid with a high-pitched voice and coke bottle glasses.

But his name *was* Seymour, and he ran the concession stand; and I didn't have to stretch my imagination very far to let myself think that that was what 'in publishing' had meant in my deja vu vision.

What the hell, I told myself, walking towards the group, who looked expectantly at me as I approached, we paranormals have to make allowances for the small mistakes. After all, it's the bigger picture that's important.

I sauntered over to the waiting group, my hands

shoved deep into my trenchcoat pockets.

'Hi, guys,' I said casually.

'You all right, Nick?' Seymour asked in a squeaky voice. 'They didn't . . . rough you up or . . . anything, did they?'

I shook my head, and noticed that he seemed as disappointed as he was relieved.

'No naked swinging light bulbs, no rubber hoses,' I assured him.

'Arresting you,' Lionel said with quiet contempt, 'what's the matter with those coppers, anyway?'

'I know,' short stout Chuck sighed. 'But they have to pin the blame on someone.'

'Maybe they should try the right man,' Lionel said drily.

'I can't believe Phil's really gone,' Chuck continued pensively. 'It seems like only yesterday I was taking him up and down.'

'It *was* yesterday,' Lionel reminded him. He looked at me. 'How'd Allison take it, Nick?'

Oh-oh, I thought, here we go: time for me to tap dance and fill in the blanks, the blanks in my knowledge, that is. But I was saved, temporarily at least, by Chuck.

'How bad could she take it?' he shrugged cynically. 'Face it, a body like that doesn't marry a guy like Phil for love.'

So Allison was Phil's wife, no, I corrected myself, make that widow. And she was apparently some sort of looker. I filed it away for future reference.

'Now that they've eliminated you, is there any real idea about who killed him?' Lionel asked. He didn't seem to have much faith in the boys in blue.

That was when the kid, Seymour piped up. 'Word on the street is that Phil was fogged by a dropper called Klapper.'

'A dropper called Klapper?' I echoed in disbelief. Was that English, I wondered?

But nobody else seemed to have any problem swimming through those murky semantic waters.

Chuck raised one eyebrow. 'Why would a dropper be after Phil?' he asked.

'Really,' I said earnestly. 'Why?'

Seymour laughed at my question, as if he thought I was poking fun at Chuck. 'You kidding?' he scoffed. 'I'll bet that between them, Phil and Nick put a dozen Hard Harrys into the slammer. And any one of 'em could have hired a dropper to fog 'em for revenge. Even from behind bars.' He paused and looked eagerly at me. 'Right Nick?'

I shrugged. 'I hope not,' I said, still picking my way through the phrasing.

'Well I hope not, too,' Lionel echoed, a worried frown creasing his brow. 'I don't need tenants with hit men after them. I've got enough problems.'

Aha! So a dropper was a hit man, just as I'd suspected. Well, almost suspected.

'Neither do I,' I assured him.

It was true: the last thing I needed was a hit man after me – I wanted to preserve Nick Allen's body and solve his problems so I could go on to . . . well, whatever it was I was scheduled to go on to next.

'So, Nick, what are you going to do?' Chuck asked.

'Do?' I repeated blankly.

'Yeah, you know. I mean, it's your job, peeper and all – you could find the guy, no sweat, right?'

'I . . . guess,' I said dubiously.

He looked a little put off by my tentative reply. 'Well, what else is there to do? Let the cops handle the investigation?'

Then, suddenly, without even thinking about it, I heard myself slipping right into tough shamus persona.

'You kidding?' I sneered and curled my lip. 'The cops? Nah, no way!' I postured and threw out attitude as if I'd been born to it.

And it had its desired effect. 'That's the way, Nick,' Seymour said with admiration.

'Yeah,' I snarled, getting into it, 'a man's partner buys it, a man knows what he has to do.' I tugged on the brim of my fedora. 'And he does it. And he doesn't stop until he nails the dropper. No matter what happens.'

'All right,' Seymour breathed.

I grabbed the nearest pulp magazine. 'Like Tommy Trueblood,' I said, indicating the cover. 'His partner was found in the Pacific sucking kelp, remember?'

'I remember,' Seymour said fervently.

I didn't even know how *I* remembered.

'Tommy had to take on the mob, the cops and the, uh, miscellaneous criminal elements.' I almost stumbled over that one. But I was on a roll. 'He risked his life, over and over,' I continued. 'He lost his girl. But did he give up? No!' I said triumphantly, 'never!'

'That's right!' Seymour, my own personal cheering section, agreed.

I couldn't seem to stop myself. 'He just kept on doing what he had to do . . . until he got . . . the dropper!' I felt as though I deserved a round of applause.

'And that's exactly what you're gonna do, Nick, right?' Seymour asked. This geeky kid had a touching amount of faith in me.

'Well . . .' I said, hedging.

Lionel shook his head. 'Uh-uh,' he interjected firmly. 'no, he's not. Not here, anyway.' He turned to me sternly. 'I don't want any more shooting here, Nick. The Gotham has a reputation to protect, and that kinda stuff frightens the tenants.'

'Not me,' Seymour said loyally.

'You don't count,' Lionel said, dismissing his opinion. 'I'm talking about paying tenants.'

'Gee . . .' Seymour said, hurt.

'Don't worry, Lionel,' I assured him. 'I'll try my best not to get shot here, OK?' I was going to try my best not to get shot *anywhere,* for that matter.

'Well . . . OK,' Lionel replied reluctantly. I had the feeling he didn't believe me, and I wondered exactly what Nick and Phil had been up to in their private investigations.

That set me thinking that it was about time to get myself into Nick's office and look around, start sniffing out clues, leads . . . well, whatever it was that private eyes sniffed out. I picked up a paper and laid fifteen cents down on the counter of the concession stand. From behind his thick glasses, Seymour stared in shock.

'Something wrong?' I asked politely.

'Uh . . . it's just, uh, that you never paid me for a paper before,' he said meekly.

Another mistake. 'Ah . . . well,' I shrugged, 'there's a first time for everything, kid.'

'. . . thanks,' Seymour said. But he still looked stunned.

I turned and sauntered towards the elevators again, needing to get away from three prying pairs of eyes. I didn't think I was doing badly as Nick Allen, Investigator, but . . .

I was halfway across the lobby when I heard something drop. 'Oh . . . shoot!' Seymour exclaimed in a squeak.

I turned back and saw that Seymour's glasses had fallen to the floor. He knelt and scrambled around, groping blindly for them and the lens which had popped out of one side of the thick black frame. I watched with curiosity as both Lionel and Chuck just stood there, exchanging knowing smiles.

Seymour managed to find the lens, but he remained

down on his knees, attempting to put it back where it belonged. He was fumbling clumsily with it.

I saw Lionel glance at his watch. 'I forget,' he said, 'what's the record?'

'Twelve minutes and eight seconds,' Chuck replied promptly.

To get a lense back into a glass frame?

'It didn't take that long,' Seymour protested, humiliated.

Jeeze, I thought, that poor kid. What an incredible, geeky nerd. And people just stood around making fun of him; it was like a scene from a grade school playground.

Lionel fished around in his pocket and pulled out a dollar bill. 'I got a buck says you can't fix it any quicker than that,' he said to Seymour.

'Hey! Make that two,' Chuck said. He glanced across the lobby to where I stood, frozen. 'Want a piece of this Nick? You're a sporting guy.'

I shook my head negatively and started for the elevators again. After all, Seymour wasn't my problem. Then, without really thinking about what I was doing, I turned around and walked back to the concession stand.

Seymour glanced up and saw me coming. His clumsy fingers got even more clumsy, and he pressed so hard on the lens that it popped up into the air again.

I reached out and caught it easily in mid-arc. Then I took the glasses gently from Seymour's hands, and snapped the lens quickly back into place. I handed them to him as he scrambled to his feet.

'You ought to get those fixed,' I told him. I didn't give a damn if it was out of character for Nick Allen, if it *was* Sam Beckett doing the deed, it was the right thing to do.

'Gee,' Seymour said humbly. 'Thanks, Nick.'

'You're welcome,' I said gruffly.

I saw the surprised looks Lionel and Chuck exchanged, the delighted smile on Seymour's face, and concluded that I was right: Nick Allen didn't go out of his way to help the underdog very often.

'Hey, Nick, wait up,' Chuck came panting after me as I reached the elevators. 'I'll take you up.'

'Okey-dokey,' I said genially. I wondered if that was tough shamus talk. I studied the headlines while we ascended to the fourth floor, and then I left the elevator in silence.

'Hey . . . Nick?' Chuck called tentatively after me.

'Yes?' I said.

He looked a little nervous. 'Uh . . . I got these tickets to the Dodger game tomorrow, you know, and, well . . .' he stopped, flushed.

So this was what hero worship was like, I thought. I was kind of touched.

'Thanks, Chuck,' I said, smiling, 'but I don't think I can make it.'

'Oh!' Chuck looked surprised. 'I didn't mean you!'

'Oh,' I said. So much for hero worship. So much for being touched.

'I was just wondering,' he continued hesitantly, 'if maybe you could ask . . . Allison. That is, if she wanted to go, I mean. To the game. You know, to take her mind off Phil's dying?'

I stared at him, aghast. 'Are you kidding?'

'Ah . . . yeah, right!' Chuck said. 'You're absolutely right. It's too soon. It's a bad idea.' He retreated and seemed to shrink into the elevator, punching buttons as he went. The elevator doors closed in front of his flushed face.

I shook my head, bemused. The day after her old

man eats the big enchilada, these guys are asking me
if I think they could ask her out? Boy, I thought,
this dame, the widow Grimsley, must be some piece of
work . . .

CHAPTER THIRTEEN

I sauntered down the dim Gotham hallway as if I'd been doing it for years. The shiny, worn linoleum and the scrubbed beige walls told the tale of a well-kept, but hardly prosperous building. The doors had the names of credit dentists, bookkeepers, low-rent theatrical publicists inscribed on them. Respectable to not-so respectable renters. And definitely not an upscale clientele.

Well, I reasoned, wasn't that what being a private eye was all about: hard knocks, low pay, personal integrity in the midst of a morally ambiguous world?

I found Nick Allen's key in his overcoat pocket, and located the door to his office. Half wood, half pebbled glass, with 'Grimsley & Allen, Discreet Investigations' neatly lettered in black. Whatever they'd been doing, it wasn't quite discreet enough, I thought – Phil had gotten himself killed, and Nick was in some kind of jam, as well. And, as an afterthought, the 'Grimsley' half of the sign on the door was going to have to go.

That thought brought me around in a circle – back to Chuck and his question, and set me wondering how he could possibly be so remarkably tasteless. I was pondering the vagaries of man's mind and just starting to fit the key to the key hole when it hit me again. That same feeling of deja vu.

I'd been here before, I'd done this before. Precisely the same way. And I knew, too, with utter certainty, that when I opened that door, I'd find someone waiting for me in that office. A chill played an arpeggio down my spine. Not just someone, but someone . . . dangerous.

I steeled myself to just keep on going: a man's gotta do what a man's gotta do, and all that stuff. I took a deep breath and turned the key in the lock and, using one tentative tap, pushed the door gently open.

It swung inward slowly. The dim office was still all black and white and dark. But there were some important differences now, a few hours after I'd leaped and landed here. One was that Phil Grimsley's body was gone, although a dark stain marked the spot of his demise. The other was the person waiting for me. As my eyes became accustomed to the lighting, I blinked. Hard.

The person waiting for me was a woman. Not just any woman. Not even just any *beautiful* woman. This was a one of a kind, a broke-the-mold model. Flaming red hair, cascading down from under a little black hat with a frivolous veil. Almond, cat-like emerald eyes, set in a creamy complexion. Full ruby lips that managed to pout and quiver and smile all at the same time. And a body . . . half-silhouetted in the light from the window, it was a body of ripe curves and long, long lines. Draped – no, molded – into somber black. Whew!

I'm no dummy. I saw the black garb, and knew immediately that this was the widow Grimsley. And just as fast that her marital status didn't matter. I swallowed. Oh, boy.

At the sight of me, Allison Grimsley dropped the smouldering cigarette she was holding into a standing ashtray, and walked across the office with a rhythm that could start the drums up in any normal jungle. She didn't pause – she just threw herself into my arms and fit there as if she'd been glued.

'Oh, Nick,' she said, with a catch in her throaty voice, 'it was so awful!'

'I know, I know,' I said soothingly, trying to give the

requisite comforting pats without getting carried away. It was a difficult task.

'Oh, Nick!' she said again, burying her face into the base of my throat. I felt my heart start to march in triple time.

I just kept doing what I was doing – patting and stroking and murmuring. But it began to get very distracting. I realized that when I'd been pondering the vagaries of man's mind, it hadn't been Chuck's mind that had done the asking.

Finally, I forced myself to pull gently away from her. Allison Grimsley sighed a deep, heartfelt sigh, and lifted the silly little veil from her face.

She looked up at me with eyes that swam with tears and honesty. 'I just couldn't stand it, Nick!'

What couldn't she stand? Phil's death?

'When I heard the police thought you killed Phillip . . .' A few strategically placed tears glistened like little diamonds on her porcelain skin.

Oh!

'Shh,' I said comfortingly, 'don't worry. It's all over now.'

'Oh, Nick! I was so afraid that they'd found out about us somehow!'

Uh-oh. Found out what? It didn't take a genius to figure out the answer to *that* one, and I felt a sinking sensation that started in my throat and moved rapidly down to my intestines.

'Oh, boy,' I said weakly.

Allison stared up at me, distressed. 'I mean . . . if they knew, it would be considered a . . . a motive to kill Phil, wouldn't it?'

'Oh, yeah,' I said, nodding in agreement. 'One of the best.'

Her wide green eyes got just a little wider. 'But . . .

you didn't, kill Phil, Nick.' She paused. 'Did you?' she said.

'No!' I said with horror, 'Of course I didn't!' At least, I certainly hoped I hadn't, or Nick hadn't. Because then this story wouldn't have a very happy ending, would it?

Allison took a deep, impressive breath, and let it out in a quivering sigh. 'Oh, Nick,' she breathed, 'I'm so glad.'

And I was glad that she was glad. Because that meant she wasn't guilty. Didn't it? Allison Grimsley made it difficult to think straight.

She placed her hands back on my shoulders. 'I just don't think I could love a man who killed my husband,' she said softly.

'No, of course not,' I agreed. It said something for her character, didn't it?

'But . . .' she looked suddenly vulnerable, frightened, 'if you didn't do it . . . who *did*?'

'Ah . . . did Phil ever happen to mention someone called Klapper?' I asked her.

'The dropper?' she replied.

Oh my God! 'You *know* him?' I asked, horrified.

'No, of course I don't,' she said, looking a little annoyed. 'How would I know a dropper?'

I shrugged. 'Maybe Phil brought his work home,' I suggested feebly.

'Actually,' Allison nibbled on her ripe lower lip thoughtfully, 'that's sort of it. One night in bed . . .' she glanced worriedly up at me, 'we slept in twin beds, you know . . .'

'Uh huh,' I said, trying not to sound as cynical as I felt. *No* red-blooded man would sleep in a separate bed if he was married to this woman.

But Allison didn't seem to notice my doubting attitude. 'Anyway,' she continued, 'one night Phillip was having a nightmare. It woke me up, because he was talking in his sleep, and he kept mumbling something about a dropper named Klapper . . .'

'Hmm,' I said.

'Is he the murderer?'

I shrugged enigmatically. 'Could be,' I said.

And then, she was back in my arms. I have to admit – physical contact with this woman wiped out a lot of doubts about her and what she was saying.

'Nick,' she murmured into my chest, 'I'm scared! I can't go back to the apartment, I just can't!'

I stroked her hair. 'Don't you have someplace else you can stay?'

She looked up at me. 'What about your place?' she asked softly.

'My place?' I echoed weakly.

Allison's green eyes glittered. 'Oh, I know – it's a little sudden and probably in very bad taste.'

No kidding, I thought.

'But the truth is Phillip is dead.' She pressed herself up against me, and I could feel the heat rising between us. 'And we've waited for so long!'

'Waited?' I repeated. Then it dawned on me. This was 1953 . . . people *didn't* necessarily hop into bed with each other at the drop of a hat. 'You mean we've never . . . '

Allison just looked puzzled.

I sighed. 'No, of course we've never. Phillip was your husband . . .'

'. . . and your partner,' Allison reminded me, 'and a man can't . . .' she let the words trail off with a coy look, but there was nothing coy about her body language.

'. . . with his partner's wife . . .' I agreed breathlessly.

'Until his partner's . . . gone,' Allison whispered.

With that, she reached down and dug around in my pants pocket. Eventually, she found my keys and I breathed a sigh of relief. Sort of. She stared up at me with a look of sly triumph, then kissed me. Really kissed me. I didn't resist.

After a while, we broke apart.

Allison dropped the keys into her purse and headed for the door. 'See you *later*,' she said meaningfully.

I dropped right into the chair behind the desk, and tilted back, gazing heavenward. 'Thank you,' I said, to whoever had sent me into this particular little adventure. 'Wow.'

I reminded myself that I was here to do a job. I pulled off my jacket, and the leather harness which held a snub-nosed .38, dumping the rig into a desk drawer. It was time to do some serious thinking. I gazed into the drawer and saw that Nick Allen had stashed a nearly empty bottle of Wild Turkey there, along with a crumpled pack of Lucky Strikes. And beneath the cigarettes lay what looked like a manuscript.

First I poured a slug of whiskey into a pleated paper dixie cup. Then, curious, I pulled the manuscript out from the drawer and flipped it open. I began to read.

'I found Phil emptying a bottle with a hand shakier than a grass skirt on Waikiki. He looked like a cat working on his ninth life ever since he heard a dropper named Klapper was looking for him.'

I sat, stunned for a moment, because those words were words I knew. That was it, I realized! All the deja vu experiences I'd been having weren't deja vu at *all*. They were familiar, predictable, because I'd *read* them – Sam Beckett had read them: I had read this book!

Aghast, I flipped through the manuscript, encountering stale similes and cut-rate Chandlerisms on every page. Some of them made me wince.

'She was a flamer,' I read aloud. 'A redhead that could

make Father Flanagan forget Boy's Town.' 'Ouch.' I shook my head.

'My first wife was a lot like that,' Al remarked as he popped into sight. He rubbed his chin thoughtfully. 'Makes me kind of wonder why we got divorced.'

'Al!' I exclaimed. 'Look at this!' I pointed to the manuscript.

'Very bad writing,' he agreed.

'No, I mean, yes it is, but that's not the point!' I said excitedly. 'This is a manuscript Nick is writing – and I read it! Published. That's why I kept having what I thought was deja vu, but it's not!'

'Thus ruining a concept way ahead of its time,' Al remarked.

I ignored his comment. 'Listen, I figured it out,' I said. 'Nick and Allison were in love, but they were too loyal to do anything about it!'

Al raised one eyebrow. 'I've seen the lady,' he said pointedly.

I waved the comment off. 'Listen,' I said, and read aloud to him. 'The heat between us was like a six day jaunt in the Sahara, but our ties to Phil were as tight as the drunk on the corner stool.'

'Whew! Not exactly Faulkner,' Al remarked.

'The thing is, this is proof, this is great! I'm here to find Phil's killer so that Allison and I can live happily ever after!'

Al's eyebrow quirked up again. 'You mean Allison and *Nick*, don't you?' he said.

'Oh . . .' I said, the realization hitting me. 'Yeah, of course.'

Al began to glance at the manuscript. 'You know, Sam,' he said conversationally, 'this Allison could turn out to be the killer.'

'Allison? No!'

'Why not?' Al asked. 'Because she's got a . . .' he began to read, 'a body that could part the Red Army?'

I reached down and slammed the manuscript shut. 'No,' I said firmly. 'Because we've got Klapper.'

Al looked aghast. 'Jeeze, Sam, you'd better be careful. They didn't have a cure for that in '53, did they?'

I sighed impatiently. 'Klapper is the dropper who shot Phil,' I told Al.

'Huh?'

'Hit man!' I said.

'Oh.' Al nodded. 'So?'

'What do you mean, "So?"' I said.

Al shrugged. 'He may have pulled the trigger, Sam, but people hire droppers, you know.'

'It wasn't Allison,' I said firmly.

'Are you thinking with your . . . brain?' Al inquired cautiously.

'This from the man who lost count of his marriages after five?' I snapped.

'That's exactly what I mean,' Al said, 'I have enough experience to see the writing on the wall!'

'Well excuse me,' I said stiffly. 'I'm not exactly a babe in the woods myself, you know.'

'How the hell do you know?' Al asked crossly. 'You can't even remember the project that started all this off!'

'Al,' I said, 'trust me.'

He snorted. 'OK, what do you want me to do?' he asked.

'I'm pretty sure that whoever the killer is, is in Nick's book. So if you can just find me a copy of . . .' I read the manuscript's title, 'Dead Men Don't Die?'

'Somehow I doubt that the thing got published under that title,' Al said.

'OK, big deal. Check under Nick Allen,' I told him.

'What if he used a nom de plume?' Al queried. 'I know I would.'

'Oh, come on!' I said. 'So what? Have Ziggy figure it out – that's what computers are for!'

'Tell Ziggy that,' Al said darkly.

I sighed. 'Al, come on. Just do it. Find this book and get it for me, because for the life of me, I can't remember how it ended!'

Al stared thoughtfully at the incomplete pages of purple prose that lay on the desk. 'It wasn't with Nick and Allison living happily ever after,' he said.

'You've read it!' I exclaimed.

'No.' Al shook his head.

'Well, then how do you know what happens?' I demanded.

'I don't know,' Al shrugged. 'But if I had to make a reasonable guess, your little scenario wouldn't really make much sense.'

'Why not?'

Al stared pointedly at me. 'Because, loverboy,' he said, 'if it ended like that, why would you need to be here? To change things to have them live *unhappily* ever after?'

'Oh,' I said, suddenly sobered. I didn't like it at all, but Al had a good point. I thought about it, and turned to him to discuss this further.

But Al was gone. He had left as suddenly and silently as he'd come.

'Damn,' I said softly.

Well, I told myself, maybe Al was right. But that was then. This was now. I had to find Phil's killer, and I was going to see to it that Allison and Nick got that chance . . . no matter what had happened in the past.

I got up and strode over to the rack where the two fedoras and two trenchcoats hung. I reached without looking, and tried to jam a too-small hat on my head.

'Must be Phil's,' I muttered, and gave a little shudder. 'Ugh.'

But the other one fit perfectly. And once again, I was properly garbed and ready to rumble. Nick Allen, detective, was on the trail.

CHAPTER FOURTEEN

I emerged back into the dim Gotham hallway with a determined attitude and a stride to match. Once again, the private eye persona was in place; once again, I was Nick Allen. Well, maybe not the writer Nick Allen – I certainly wouldn't want to lay claim to *that* – but the shamus Nick Allen. And if I couldn't have Allison Grimsley for myself, I'd have her for Nick. No, wait a minute, I thought, I didn't mean it like that. Or did I?

She certainly was a girl to set the imagination running and the hormones flaring. I couldn't remember anybody, or any *body*, who had ever had quite the effect on me that Allison Grimsley was having. But then again, as Al had so snidely reminded me, I couldn't remember much of anything at all.

'Nick!' Seymour's squeaky voice, pitched higher than usual with obvious excitement, interrupted my mental meanderings.

'Huh?' I replied, as he came rushing in my direction from the elevator. I was still contemplating a mental picture of Allison Grimsley.

I noticed offhandedly that Seymour's thick glasses were tilted slightly askew, and his face was bright with anticipation – sort of like an over eager puppy, I thought unkindly.

'Nick!' he repeated. 'Guess what? You're never going to believe this!'

'Believe what?'

'I've got a lead on the Klapper!'

'You do?' I said with amazement. He was right, it was hard for me to believe. I had a hard time believing Seymour could even brush his *teeth* without help, let alone turn up a clue in a murder investigation.

'He's going to be at the Blue Island tonight!' Seymour exclaimed.

'The . . . oh, the Blue Island. Yeah, I read . . .' I caught myself just in time, 'I mean, Phil told me about the Blue Island.' I looked curiously at Seymour. 'But how did you hear about it?' I asked.

Seymour fell into stride beside me, man to man. He lowered his voice, talking in a confidential, man-to-man tone. 'I got tipped by a kid who works there – we were in the orphanage together.'

The orphanage? Oh, come on, I thought! Jeeze, this kid was like something out of a work of fiction himself. 'And?' I said.

'And what?'

I looked at him impatiently. 'Did he tell you how we'd know it was Klapper? Exactly what we were supposed to look for?'

Seymour sighed. 'Well . . .' he said reluctantly, 'he couldn't . . . or *wouldn't* give me a face. No description at all. Just the name, and the information that he'll be there.'

'How are we supposed to find him if we don't know what he looks like?' I sighed.

'I thought of that!' Seymour said. He actually looked proud of himself. 'We'll do it the same way Tommy Trueblood did in "The Lipstick Murders," remember?'

'Oh, sure,' I said gloomily.

'Yeah!' Seymour said, excited by the idea. 'We'll pose as a couple of moustaches who want to offer him a contract.' He looked at me, eager for approval.

I nodded, although I thought the idea of Seymour

getting away with posing as anything other than the geeky kid he really *was* was pretty amusing. And I wasn't absolutely certain, but I had an idea that moustaches meant Mafioso, and Seymour as a Mafioso was beyond amusing, it was mind-boggling.

'So, Nick . . . got your Roscoe?' Seymour asked in a hushed tone.

'Roscoe?' I repeated.

Seymour looked at me oddly. 'Your piece. Your gat. Shooter.'

'Oh. My gun,' I said. Of course. 'No,' I lied, 'the police confiscated it.' The truth was that I had purposely left it in the office – I had no intention of carrying or using a gun. Under any circumstances.

'Oh.' Seymour looked momentarily disappointed, but he brightened up immediately. 'That's OK, Nick,' he said, 'we've always got our dukes. Right?'

'Oh, sure,' I said. 'Right.'

The doors slid open as we approached the elevator. Buoyed by my response, Seymour ducked and feinted, then threw a playful jab in my direction.

I just as playfully ducked the punch and stepped into the elevator. Only . . . there was no elevator!

'Oh, my God!' I yelled as I teetered on the brink of space. 'Oh, Christ!'

My arms began to windmill reflexively, as I attempted to keep my balance, to keep from plunging off the ledge which separated me from the elevator shaft.

'Seymour!' I screamed. 'Do something!'

Seymour seemed to be frozen in place, paralyzed by fright and unable to come to my rescue. I could see his eyes bugging out behind his glasses. I could see his mouth opening in a feeble scream. But he couldn't move.

'Ahhh . . .' I yelled.

Finally, I was unable to maintain my balance any

longer. There didn't seem to really be a choice: I gave up and pushed myself off into space, grabbing for the cable which held the elevator car. Tarzan like, I just managed to get ahold of it. The twisted cable precariously slippery in my grasp, I launched my body out into the empty space of the shaft. For a breath-taking moment I just hung there, suspended over space, and then, in a taut circle, I swung gently back to the fourth floor landing.

'Jesus!' I gasped in relief, as my feet touched firm floor again. 'Jesus!' I could feel my heart pounding like crazy. I grabbed the frame of the elevator door and clung to it.

I looked over at Seymour, who still appeared to be rooted in place. His face was pale and sweaty, and before my very eyes, he just crumpled up and fell to the floor in an unconscious heap.

'Great,' I muttered. 'A would-be detective who faints at the sight of danger.' I looked down at his prostrate form and sighed. 'You poor idiot,' I said.

Then I stepped around Seymour and headed for the stairs, the safe route, to fetch the elevator operator and the building superintendent. How, I wondered, could this have happened?

*   *   *

'This just can't happen!' Lionel exclaimed, his voice shaking, as he examined the open elevator door. Nearby, looking equally shaken by the near-accident, were Chuck, and the now-conscious Seymour. 'This just isn't possible – it can't happen!'

'Well, it did,' I said pragmatically. At this point, I seemed to be the only calm one in the bunch. I pointed to the space before us.

'But the doors won't open unless the elevator is there.' Lionel said firmly.

Nothing like refuting reality, I thought.

'But they did,' I said stubbornly. After all, I'd nearly bought the farm, thereby, at the very least, earning the right to disagree with the man.

'It *can* happen,' Chuck said timidly.

Lionel whirled on him. 'How?' he demanded. 'What are you talking about?'

'The doors can open if the safety latch is broken,' Chuck informed us.

'Broken?' Lionel said. 'What do you mean, broken? How can the safety latch be broken?'

Chuck shrugged defensively. 'It just happens,' he said.

'It just happens?' I echoed. It sounded pretty feeble to me.

Lionel looked apoplectic. 'Then this is all your fault!' he yelled.

'It is not!' Chuck yelled back. 'It's yours! I told you again and again that this elevator was old, that it needed to be replaced!'

'You never said anything about it being deadly!' Lionel fumed. 'My God, I'm liable for anything that happens here . . . I could lose my job, I could get sued . . .'

'Maybe if you listened to me once in a while . . .'

I sighed and gave up. I doubted there were going to be any cogent answers to this puzzle forthcoming here. These guys were too busy trying to pass the buck back and forth to really try to get to the bottom of it all.

'Come on,' I said to Seymour. 'Let's take a hike.'

He joined me happily, and we headed for the stairs, while behind us, Lionel and Chuck continued to argue over who was responsible for the elevator problem. They didn't even seem to notice our departure.

We pushed open the heavy metal door which led to the stairway, and as it whooshed shut behind us, Seymour

133

glanced around, as if making sure we were out of earshot. Or danger.

'Nick!' he whispered.

'What?' I said absentmindedly. I was preoccupied with my own thoughts.

'Klapper did it!'

'Did what?'

'Nick!' Seymour hissed. 'He tried to kill you!'

I looked at him seriously. 'You don't have to whisper, Seymour,' I told him. 'There's no-one around. And besides, I seriously doubt that Klapper had anything to do with what just happened.'

'Why not?' He looked positively disappointed, but he spoke in a normal tone.

'Because Klapper's a professional, and pro's rarely miss,' I said tersely.

'Oh,' Seymour said, deflated.

'Besides,' I added sensibly, 'think about it for a minute. How could he possibly be sure I'd be the one to use the elevator next, or that I'd just walk blindly into it? There are too many ifs, and ifs don't add up to a dropper's M.O.'

Seymour looked chagrined. 'That was my fault,' he said. 'I distracted you. I'm always getting in the way,' he added.

I sighed. 'It wasn't your fault,' I said. 'I should have looked first.'

But Seymour had found a theme, and he seemed to want to stick with it. 'I'm always getting in the way,' he said sadly. 'I've been causing accidents since I was born – probably before. That's probably why my folks dumped me to begin with.'

'You were abandoned?' I said, feeling a sudden pang of guilt for having been so impatient with him.

Seymour nodded morosely. 'Left on a stoop in the East

134

Village,' he said. 'I grew up in the East End Orphanage.'
He sighed. 'Mostly in the library.'

'What's wrong with liking to read?' I asked, trying to
inject a cheery note to this depressing turn in the conversation.

'I slept there,' Seymour informed me. 'It was the only
place no-one would bother me.'

'Oh.' I was at a loss for words. It was all too painfully
easy to picture a pitiful, miniature Seymour bullied and
beaten up by the bigger boys. And it wasn't a pretty
picture.

'I wish I could be just like you,' Seymour said wistfully.

'Oh, come on! A two-bit detective who deals in divorce
cases?' I scoffed. Somebody had to shake this kid out of
a bad case of misplaced hero worship.

'Don't say that!' Seymour said fervently. 'You're Nick
Allen! You're . . . the best!'

'That's what I've always said.' The voice came from
the landing below us, and the throaty growl was un-
mistakable.

Seymour and I stared down at Allison Grimsley, who
stared back. Somewhere between the time she'd left my
office and now, she'd lost the veil – along with any
semblance of a widow's mournful attitude – and she was
doing things to a cigarette that were positively startling.
Not to mention suggestive.

'Oh, boy,' Seymour and I sighed in unison.

'Is something wrong?' Allison asked innocently. Well,
not precisely innocently.

'Sorry, Mrs Grimsley,' Seymour gulped. 'I just never
saw a widow who looked like you before.'

Allison pouted. 'Is it my fault if black happens to be
a good color for me?'

'Ahh . . .' said Seymour.

'Besides,' Allison said, throwing an up-from-under look in my direction, 'I hadn't really planned on keeping this outfit on . . . later.'

'Oh, boy,' I whispered.

'Nick,' Seymour said, glancing down at his watch, 'look what time it is. We've got to go!'

I wasn't sure if he was trying to save me from myself, or if he was just too naive to figure out what Allison was not so subtly implying. I looked at him, and decided it was the latter. Poor kid.

'Go?' Allison said. 'Go where?'

'We've got a lead!' Seymour said eagerly.

'You do?' Allison was looking at me.

'Yeah!' Seymour bungled on enthusiastically before I could stop him. 'We do! We're going to the Blue Island to track it down!'

Allison's expression changed from inviting to worried. 'Oh, no!' she exclaimed. 'No! You can't go there!'

I looked at her suspiciously. Why was she so insistent, I wondered. 'Why not?' I asked.

'God, Nick! You know why – that's where Phillip went the night before he died!' Her green eyes were pleading with me.

But that just made me more suspicious. 'Why didn't you tell me that?' I asked pointedly.

'Nick, what on earth are you talking about?' Allison asked, looking completely bewildered. 'Tell you what? You went with him!'

Oops. 'Of course I did,' I said matter of factly.

Thank heaven, I thought, Seymour hadn't noticed my gaffe before, when I told him I'd heard about the Blue Island from Phil.

Allison studied me with worried eyes. 'OK, what's wrong?' she said finally.

'Nothing,' I said.

'He's a little shook up,' Seymour chimed in by way of explanation. 'He nearly fell down an elevator shaft and died.'

'What!' Allison exclaimed, horrified.

'It was my fault,' Seymour added.

God, this kid could yack. 'It wasn't your fault,' I said patiently. 'It was an accident.'

Allison's eyes narrowed. 'Whoever murdered Phillip is after you, Nick, isn't he?' she demanded. Well, her deductive powers seemed to be in working order.

'Well . . .' I hedged. 'I don't think we necessarily have to see it that way . . .'

'Klapper's a pro,' Seymour said seriously to Allison.

'Is there an echo in this stairwell?' I murmered.

'. . . and he knows the code,' Seymour continued firmly.

'So?' Allison said.

'So . . . whether or not it was the Klapper, Nick won't stop tracking his crushers until they're pushing up daisies in Potter's Field.'

'I don't know if I follow that, exactly,' Allison said, puzzled.

I shrugged. 'Me neither,' I admitted.

Allison moved sinuously halfway up the stairs toward us. It was a different view of that black-clad body that drove men wild. I noticed that not only was the veil gone, but the top three buttons of her very fitted jacket had been undone.

'Nick,' she said softly.

'Uh-huh?' I said. Beside me, Seymour sighed.

'Nick, if you really care for . . . Phillip,' Allison said, looking meaningfully at me, 'you won't do anything stupid. You won't risk your life unnecessarily, because if you get killed, then who will keep his memory alive? Who will solve his murder?'

Seymour was probably aching to volunteer for duty, but he had the presence of mind not to volunteer – either that, or he didn't have the nerve.

'Allison,' I said firmly, 'a man's gotta do what a man's gotta do. And when a man's partner gets killed, you know what a man's gotta do.'

Allison Grimsley's eyes filled with tears. 'Nick,' she pleaded, 'don't do it – don't go to the Blue Island. Please?'

Turning her down was the hardest thing I'd ever done. 'I have to,' I told her. 'You want me to find Phillip's killer, don't you?'

Allison's eyes were suddenly hooded and mysterious. I couldn't have said what she was thinking just then. I wasn't sure I wanted to know.

'All right,' she conceded, finally.

I breathed a sigh of relief.

'But . . . just one thing,' she added.

'What's that?' I asked.

'You're not going there alone,' she said.

'Oh, don't worry, Mrs Grimsley,' Seymour piped up, 'I'll be there with Nick.'

She smiled vaguely in his direction, then turned her high powered beams back on me. 'That's not what I meant,' she said.

'Then what . . .' I let the words trail off. I had a feeling I knew what was coming next.

'I'm going with you,' she said firmly.

'No . . .' I began.

'Yes,' she said. She looked utterly determined. 'I have every right to be there when you . . . do what you've gotta do.'

I couldn't argue that point. Not at all.

CHAPTER FIFTEEN

The Blue Island was a big, classy joint, jumping with good cheer and friendly sounds. The nightclub had a couple of bustling bars serving exotic concoctions in pineapples and coconuts, as well as the standard stuff; there was a large, polished and well attended dance floor, and loads of ambience.

The owners had gone all out to create a distinct mood, a sort of tropical island retreat from the everyday cares of busy Manhattan life.

The banquettes and tables were upholstered in soft leather, the tables had colorful, patterned linen cloths, bright with parrots and fruit and flowers – the kind you wouldn't ever see on Long Island – and the lighting was soft and purposely intimate. Little star lights glittered from the ceiling, and on the tables, the soft glow came from bulbs cunningly hidden under whimsical plastic fruit arrangements.

The clientele matched the place: upscale, dressed to the nines, reeking of good times. Men wore tuxedos, women wore floor length evening dresses and lots of sparkling jewels and furs. There was an air of perfume and money and retreat from the little everyday bothers of life. Even the band was formally clad, and they played all the standard classics of the day, going from up-beat to smokey and back again. The whole thing was . . . well, it was the fifties at their glamorous best. I liked it.

And we fit right in. In Nick Allen's cramped Midtown

bachelor pad, I'd found a white tuxedo. And I had to admit, it looked great. Although I *also* had to admit that who it actually looked great on was Nick Allen, or Bogey. Not Sam Beckett. And Allison looked, well, smashing was the only word.

She was still in black – either a concession to her recent widowhood, or, as she had mentioned earlier, because she just looked good in it. Her shiny taffeta gown was strapless and practically backless, and it looked as if it had been spray painted on her; it was a near miracle that it stayed up. In stilletto heels and a little fox wrap thrown carelessly over one bare white shoulder, she was enough to set a blind man drooling as she sauntered easily through the crowd.

Seymour, of course, was a different matter. I glanced over at him, where he sat at a table talking to his 'source.' It was a little unnerving, because the source was a busboy who looked enough like Seymour to be his twin brother. He was just as young, just as skinny, just as nervous and pimply. I wondered what they fed them at that orphanage.

I was distracted by the sight of Allison moving my way. As I watched her sashay back from a visit to the powder room, I couldn't help noticing the way other men looked at her. She was beautiful, all right, but there were a lot of beautiful women in the Blue Island. It was something different, it was more than beauty. Allison had a quality that incited pure animal lust in men. I could well imagine that men would be willing to do anything, even commit murder, to win her.

Along that same uncomfortable line, I had formulated two theories about why Allison had insisted that she come with me to the night club. One was that she was guilty: she had hired Klapper to kill Phil, and she wanted to be on the spot to make sure that I didn't find him. The other was . . . that she really loved me. Nick Allen, that is, I corrected myself. She really loved Nick Allen. And that she was here because she was genuinely frightened for his safety.

Guess which theory I wanted to believe?

'Dance with me,' she murmured, dropping bag and wrap on the table.

I obligingly took her into my arms, and sighed as she snuggled in.

'Oh, Nicky,' she said softly, 'I probably should be frightened, but it's hard . . .'

I started to blush.

'. . . to feel anything but safe in your arms.'

'You are safe,' I assured her, although I wouldn't have laid money on it.

She snuggled in even closer, every curve fitting neatly up against me. I could smell the heady fragrance of the gardenia she wore pinned in her hair. We stood there and just sort of swayed to the music.

Safe, however, *wasn't* a word I'd use about the way Allison Grimsley made *me* feel. She was like a waving red flag, a howling siren, a storm warning. But, oh, how she felt. I pulled her in even more tightly. Hell, I thought, why not just go with the flow? Why look a gift . . . whatever, in the mouth?

Just then, I opened my eyes, and over the top of Allison's head, I spotted Al. He was standing right next to the band leader, tapping out time to the music, and looking like he was enjoying himself immensely. He winked and waved at me.

I guess I must have stiffened, because Allison pulled back a little and stared up at me. 'What's wrong?' she asked.

'Nothing,' I said.

'You've spotted him, haven't you?' she demanded.

Oh no, I thought, how could she possibly know? 'What? Who?' I asked nervously.

'Klapper,' she said in a dramatic whisper.

'Oh! No.' I smiled at her, relieved. 'No, I just thought I recognized an . . . old client. From a messy divorce case.'

'Oh,' Allison breathed. 'Good.' Then she added thoughtfully, 'Thank God I didn't have to go through that.' She gasped as she realized what she'd said. 'Oh, Nick! I didn't mean that the way it sounded, you have to believe me!'

'Don't worry about it,' I said soothingly. 'You're just distraught.'

I glanced back over her head at Al again. He pulled a paperback from his tux pocket and held it up for me to see. He'd gotten it!

Allison read my body language again, and turned her head to see what I was staring at. 'You *do* see him, don't you?' she said. She looked up at me, her green eyes frightened.

'Ah . . . no, Allison.' I nodded in Al's direction. 'Honest. I'm just . . . distracted.' Right. 'Listen, let's take a break, OK?'

And without really giving her a chance to protest, I steered her off the floor and over towards the table where Seymour still sat.

But Allison wasn't a woman who gave up that easily. 'You're hiding something,' she said. 'I know you are! Klapper's in the band, isn't he?' she insisted. 'Damn it, Nick, tell me!'

If she was faking her distress, she was a damned good actress. But, a little voice insisted, that wasn't hard to believe, either. As we reached the table, Seymour leaped to his feet and pulled out a chair for her.

'Tell me!' she demanded again.

142

'Allison, how can I spot someone when I don't know what he looks like?' I said patiently.

'Who?' said Seymour.

'Klapper!' Allison said, biting her lip. 'He's here!'

'He may look like a she,' said Seymour.

'What?' I said.

'*What*?' Allison said.

Seymour nodded. 'New whisper on the street says the Klapper's a woman,' he said dramatically.

I glanced over at Allison, who appeared to be studying the tablecloth. It was an unsettling thought, although, for some reason, it didn't surprise me. The conversation seemed to come to a standstill.

'I think I'll go and get us some fresh drinks,' I said finally.

'I'll get them, Nick,' Seymour volunteered.

'You stay here and keep Allison company,' I told him. I wanted to get to Al and find out what the hell was happening.

'Sure!' Seymour said enthusiastically. 'Great!'

Allison looked up and threw me an enigmatic look. She pulled a cigarette from her beaded black evening bag, and Seymour practically fell over himself lighting it for her.

'Thanks,' she said smokily.

As I walked away, I heard him say, 'Did you ever read Tommy Trueblood?'

I maneuvered my way around the crowded dance floor and over to a dark corner of the bar where Al and I could talk without being observed. Where I could talk seemingly to myself, that is, without being observed.

'Wow, Sam,' Al said admiringly as he slid on to the bar stool next to mine, 'that Allison Grimsley is a stone killer!'

'Nick *wrote* that?' I demanded. 'Are you sure?'

'Nick?' Al looked puzzled.

'The book,' I reminded him impatiently.

'Oh, the book!' He snapped his fingers. 'Right. No, I meant her body. Deadly, Sam, just deadly.' He peeked through the fronds of a potted palm. 'You know, she kind of reminds me of that redhead in Billing, the one who . . .'

'Al!' I said impatiently. I didn't want to hear it. 'So help me, if you start to tell me another one of your sleazy sex stories, I swear, hologram or no hologram, I'll slug you!'

Al paused. 'Sleazy?' he said. He looked almost offended.

'Sleazy,' I told him firmly.

Al sniffed. 'You know, Sam,' he said haughtily, 'there's sleaze, and then, there's . . . sleaze!'

I snorted. 'I don't have time for this. Just tell me who killed Phil!' I hissed.

Al shrugged. 'I don't know,' he said.

'What do you mean you don't know?' I snapped. 'You've got the book! Didn't you read it?'

'Yeah, but it's an unfinished story,' Al informed me. 'It's what was called a contest book – they were very popular back in the fifties. They were true crimes, unsolved ones, and the readers had to finish the story . . .'

I groaned. 'Great,' I said. 'Just my luck.' Then I glanced down at the paperback.

'The whole thing was to figure out the murderer and if the cops could prove it, you won ten grand.' He rubbed his chin thoughtfully. 'That was a lot of dough in those days,' he said.

'Al,' I said, staring. '*Look* at this – the title is "Who killed Grimsley and Allen"! By Rock Roscoe!'

'Yeah,' Al agreed. 'I don't get it – Nick Allen is a much better name than Rock Roscoe.'

'I think I'm a little more concerned about the title than the pseudonym!' I said.

'I thought you'd get around to noticing that.'

'Here you go,' the bartender said, 'two Martinis extra dry, and a Shirley Temple. Three dollars.'

I put a five down on the bar and the man moved away, smiling happily.

'What a rip-off,' Al observed. 'It's 1953, Sam. Any downtown bar would charge a buck and a quarter. Tops. And you tipped him too much.'

I didn't feel like chatting about bar etiquette. I took a sip of my Martini, which was just right, and turned to Al. 'How did I . . . Nick, I mean, die?' I asked him bluntly.

'Back-stopped an ounce of lead.'

God, he was talking like Seymour. 'Was it Klapper?' I asked.

'Probably,' Al said. 'But no-one ever collected on it.'

I pointed to the book. 'Who did the readers suspect?'

Al smiled cynically. 'Everyone from Joseph Stalin to Colonel Mustard in the kitchen with a rope. But the majority of the folks seemed to agree.' He looked meaningfully at me.

'Agree to what?' I said, although I had a sinking feeling I knew what was coming.

'They tended to vote for . . .' he swiveled around and peered through the potted palm again, '. . . the red widow.'

I didn't care if it was the same direction my own suspicions had been leading me in – I didn't want to hear it from Al. 'But they never proved anything, did they?' I demanded.

Al stared me straight in the eye. 'They couldn't prove anything, Sam. Because she and Seymour disappeared the night of Nick's murder.'

'Which was . . .' I looked meaningfully at him.

He nodded. 'Tonight.'

I sagged on my barstool. This was getting worse by the minute. 'Allison and Seymour?' I said in disbelief.

Al nodded. 'Are you sure?' I said weakly.

Al nodded again, then shrugged. 'Like I said, nothing was ever proved one way or the other. But they both disappeared without a trace, on the same night. Rumor was that they flew off to Rio.'

'Together?' I said, still having a hard time digesting it.

'Together,' he said.

'I don't believe it,' I said stoutly.

Al peered through the palm again. 'It does stretch the imagination pretty much right up to the breaking point, doesn't it?' he agreed. 'I mean, just look at her. Look at him! What on earth would she *do* with him?'

'Oh, come on,' I said. I didn't want to hear this, not at all.

'But then again,' Al shrugged, promptly reversing himself, 'some women do have kinky taste in men. Thank God.'

I ignored his ramblings and searched for another explanation, *any* other explanation. 'Al!' I exclaimed happily. 'I think I've got it!'

'What?' he asked. 'What Allison would do with Seymour?'

'No,' I said impatiently. 'I think I know what really happened. I bet Klapper killed both of *them*, too, and then he hid their bodies where they'd never be found.'

'The old cement shoes in the East River trick?' Al asked sarcastically.

'Maybe,' I insisted.

'Not a chance,' Al said firmly.

'Why not?' I replied querulously.

'Well, for one thing,' Al said mildly, 'it doesn't make

much sense. Phil Grimsley's body was left in his office. Nick Allen's body was left at LaGuardia. Think about it, Sam. If Klapper left the two of *them* where he killed them, why would he bother to hide Allison and Seymour?'

I pondered for a moment. 'I don't know,' I admitted finally, 'but it's the only logical explanation.' I wasn't about to relinquish my theory so easily. Especially because it absolved Allison of any culpability in the killings. Although, come to think of it, it left her dead in the process.

Al shook his head. 'No, it's not the only logical explanation,' he argued. 'A far more logical one is that Allison is the Klapper.'

'I don't believe that,' I said stubbornly.

'Oh, come on, Sam,' Al scoffed. 'Look at her – to have safe sex with that broad, you'd have to be wearing a bullet proof vest!'

'Al,' I said warningly. I didn't like where his mind was going.

'Oh, well,' he shrugged, still staring at Allison and Seymour across the room, 'maybe you're right.'

'Now you're using your . . .' I began.

But Al didn't give me a chance to finish. 'A body like that,' he observed, 'couldn't be interested in Seymour no matter how kinky her Id is.' He nodded thoughtfully. 'She must have just used the dopey kid until she didn't need him anymore, and then blown him away. Maybe in Rio, after all.'

I felt my anger rising. 'Allison didn't blow anyone away!' I insisted.

'How do you know?' Al shot the question at me, his dark eyes bright and inquisitive and . . . disbelieving.

'I just . . . know,' I said. 'Call it instinct.'

Al bit back a laugh. 'I guess that's one word for it, Pal.

But *my* instincts tell me that Allison Grimsley has you tied up tighter than a Christmas package, and you haven't got the slightest idea . . .'

'Shut up, Al,' I seethed. 'Who the hell are you to talk? Your instincts got you married five times!'

Al looked a little hurt by the pointed comment. '*That* your Swiss cheese brain remembers!'

I sat in sullen silence, nursing my Martini.

'Sam,' Al said more gently, 'I know it's been awhile since you got any . . .'

That did it. I wasn't going to sit here and listen to this any more. 'Don't compare me to yourself,' I said icily. 'I think with my brain, not the other parts of my anatomy.'

'Sam!' Al said, shocked.

I couldn't seem to stop myself. 'And I don't cloud my judgement with anything that comes in a bottle!'

There was a sudden weighty, dead silence. It was as if all noise in the room had somehow faded into ambient background sound, and there was just Al and me, and . . . silence. I didn't even want to look at him; I knew that last remark had stung. But I was still angry.

Finally, Al spoke. 'Gotta go,' he said, keeping his tone light. 'Tina's waiting. Our tip – remember that horse I was telling you about? It's running in the eighth. Nostalgia Kills. Funny name, isn't it? Even for a filly.'

I gave a tight-lipped nod, and stared into the drink in front of me.

'Sam?' Al said.

I looked up. 'What?' My voice was still terse.

'Just do me a favor, kid. If you've gotta fly tonight, fly out of Newark, Idlewild . . . any place but LaGuardia. OK?'

I nodded reluctantly.

'Adios,' Al said, his eyes dark and serious.

148

'Al . . .' I began impulsively, but he was already gone through that door that took him . . . wherever it took him. He was gone and I felt like a complete heel.

I sat there for a few minutes, nursing my drink and brooding. I knew my theory didn't really hold water: there wasn't even any reason for Klapper to kill Allison and Seymour, presuming he'd killed Grimsley and Allen for revenge in the first place. I knew in my heart of hearts that there was a damned good chance that Al was right. Dead right.

I felt like slamming my fist into the bar, but I controlled the urge. I wondered why it was that we inevitably hurt people who told us the truths we didn't want to hear.

I peered through the palm fronds the way Al had done. I could see Allison lighting another cigarette, Seymour babbling on and on, trying to amuse her. Through the haze of the club, she was incredibly desirable. And I knew then and there that Al was absolutely right about *one* thing: when it came to Allison Grimsley, I was as blind as a dead bat, and tighter than a granny knot at a Cub Scout competition.

Oh, my God, I thought, I'm thinking the way Seymour talks! I was horrified. It was time to get back into action.

I took fresh drinks and my unpleasant new knowledge back to the table, where Seymour was continuing to regale a bored looking Allison with tales of Tommy Trueblood.

'So this pin jabber tried to fog him with a stick of nitro, but Tommy smelled the blow, and he creased the horse rider with an ounce of lead.'

Allison looked up at me pleadingly.

'Let's blow this pop stand,' I said.

'OK, Nick!' Seymour said eagerly.

'Thank God,' said Allison under her breath.

149

She gathered up her wrap and bag, and the three of us made our way across the dance floor and towards the door. As we passed by the bandstand, I saw the band leader smile in delighted recognition. I smiled back, and he motioned off to the side.

Then the spot light hit me.

'Oh, no,' I murmured. I had forgotten.

The band broke into 'As Time Goes By.' Everyone in the crowd began to applaud. I smiled uncomfortably and waved, then hurried off the floor. As I reached the door, where Seymour and Allison waited for me, Seymour looked at me admiringly.

'God, Nick,' he said, awed, 'it's so neat! Everyone thinks Bogie looks like you!'

I sighed. 'I think you have it backwards,' I said.

'Huh?' Seymour looked puzzled.

'Never mind,' I told him.

Jeeze.

CHAPTER SIXTEEN

'Just keep walking,' I muttered to Allison and Seymour, keeping a resolutely fixed, uncomfortable grin on the face that everyone thought was Bogie's.

'Right, Nick, good thinking,' Seymour agreed, scurrying on ahead. 'It's not a good idea to draw too much attention, not even if they think they're peeping at another shamus, the smokescreen kind.'

'Yeah, yeah,' I said, too embarrassed to even try to wend my way through Seymour's lingo. I wondered how celebrities lived with this kind of nonsense happening all the time.

We pushed hurriedly through the padded, buttoned leather doors of the club and I took a deep breath of relief as we came out into the night; but I could hear the strains of the orchestra playing 'As Time Goes By,' still following us.

It was an uncomfortable reminder that not only wasn't I *myself*, I wasn't even who I *wasn't* supposed to be. Wait a minute, I thought, this is getting too confusing . . .

Still, if this was what happened to the real Nick Allen every time he went out in public, I thought, his life must be a living hell. He'd have to spend half his time fending off admirers. Not to mention the fact that looking like Humphrey Bogart was hardly a way to keep a low profile. How could you conduct surveillance? How could you not blow your gumshoe cover? How could you possibly tail somebody in obscurity if people were always asking you for your autograph?

We stood under the striped canvas awning that stretched protectively from the double doors of the Blue Island all the way to the curb of the street, watching traffic on 58th St, while the busy doorman raced halfway down the block trying to scare up cabs for another group of nightclub customers who had emerged just before we did.

The city streets were crowded with well dressed pedestrians and thick noisy traffic. A rainbow assortment of flashing neon lights cast a moody, intermittent glow over the scene.

Just another bustling, Manhattan night I mused silently. No different for most people than any other busy night in the city. Except that this was the night that Nick Allen was slated to buy the farm, and I had to make sure that didn't happen.

Seymour was still hopped up from his encounter with the glamorous life. 'Do you think that Bogie copies you?' he asked me eagerly. 'Maybe he gets his best screen shamus moves from your cases.'

'Like real life imitating art?' I asked, distracted. 'I doubt it.'

Allison gave me a peculiar look. 'What did you say?' she asked.

I slapped myself mentally, reminding myself to try to stay in character. Maybe Nick Allen didn't talk that way. *Probably* Nick Allen didn't talk that way. But I didn't have time to worry about verisimilitude now, I had a bigger problem to solve.

'Exactly!' Seymour said. He didn't seem to notice the difference in speech pattern.

'No,' I shook my head. 'I don't even think he knows that I exist.'

Seymour looked disappointed. Then he perked up. 'I don't know,' he said, hopefully, 'after all, Nick, you're pretty famous.'

The kid's ongoing state of awe and respect was positively unnerving, I thought. There didn't seem to be any way to keep his admiration in check.

Then I was distracted as I felt a strong gust of wind shake up the canvas of the awning. It was followed by a flash of lightning that lit up the sky. Beside me, Allison snuggled up close.

'Wow,' said Seymour, peering up at the sky from under the awning.

A moment later, a clap of thunder sounded, a reverberating boom!

Allison shivered. 'It's going to pour,' she said, peering out into the streaming traffic. 'Where's that doorman?'

But he was nowhere to be seen. Allison shivered again.

'You two just wait here,' Seymour told us, always ready to oblige. 'I'll be able to flag down a cab for us over on Madison.'

'Seymour . . .' I began. 'You don't have to run out – it's going to rain, and we can just wait here until . . .'

'No, it's OK, I'd rather be doing something useful . . .' he said, and then he was gone, disappearing into the crowd of people now hurrying to get someplace before the storm broke.

'Jesus,' I muttered. 'That kid . . .'

'Oh, never mind him,' Allison murmured, cuddling closer.

Never mind him, I thought, uh-huh. Sure. Never mind the geeky kid who is rumored to have disappeared with you, Allison. The night of my – Nick's – murder. Never mind Rio. Never mind the ideas that Al had put into my head about your culpability.

Beside me, Allison had wrapped her arm around mine and laid her head on my shoulder. But she seemed to sense my preoccupation.

'Nick?' she said softly. 'What's wrong? What are you thinking about?'

Without really considering the words, I said the first thing that popped into my head. 'Allison, did you love Phil?'

Allison tugged abruptly away from me and stared up into my somber face. 'What kind of question is that?' she asked evenly. Her catlike eyes were calm, her voice steady.

I couldn't tell if she felt offended or she was simply surprised.

'The kind of question that has to be asked,' I told her solemnly.

Allison sighed. 'The code?' she asked.

I nodded.

'I suppose you're right,' she said, after a pause in which she seemed to reflect. 'It's just that it's something I don't really think about, haven't wanted to talk about. It's the past. And . . . it was all such a long time ago, Nick.'

'But . . . it's a past that I need to know about,' I insisted.

Allison sighed again, then nodded. 'OK, you have the right to know. But it's not very interesting. It's certainly not an *original* story,' she told me. 'Not by any stretch of the imagination.'

I shrugged. 'That's OK,' I told her. 'Try me.'

A bitter smile tugged briefly at her lips. 'I was only sixteen when I met Phil,' she said. 'Just a . . . baby, really.'

I could picture Allison at sixteen, and I had a feeling that the baby had been the kind of jail bait which came wrapped in a very enticing package, the kind that could make you forget the consequences of unwrapping it.

'He was in Pittsburgh, working on a divorce case,' Allison continued. 'One afternoon, he wandered in for coffee. I was slinging hash after school at a neighborhood diner.'

In a tight rayon uniform, I thought. Oh, boy. I resolutely pushed the mental image away.

'I guess you could say he swept me off my feet,' Allison went on. 'After all, I didn't know anything about anything, and he seemed so . . . I don't know, so sophisticated.' She smiled ruefully. 'An older man, a private eye. From New York! It was all so glamorous sounding, at least, to me.'

No, it certainly wasn't an original story, I thought. That much was true. 'So . . . you did love him,' I ventured. 'Sort of?'

Allison shrugged, a sad little smile tugging at her lips. 'I think I loved the *idea* of him,' she admitted. 'You have to try to understand, Nick – I was the daughter of a steel worker. To put it mildly, my outlook on life was limited.'

I nodded thoughtfully.

'I'd never been anywhere outside of my own neighborhood,' Allison said, 'and I didn't really ever expect to *go* anywhere else! And then there was Phil, and he seemed to be offering me this whole new world. And . . . well, I felt like if I didn't grab the chance to go with him, I'd never get another opportunity!'

'So you went,' I said.

'Of course I did,' she said candidly. 'And I've never regretted it. I wasn't meant to be a steel town drudge! And I'm a quick study.'

I could understand what she was saying. A young, provincial girl, a girl who lacked skills – except the blatantly obvious one – but a girl who was bright and eager and pretty. With her background, what choices did she have?

I could imagine that young Allison, sniffed after by local teenage boys and hefty, sullen steel workers, clones

155

of her father. Not seeing any other chance in life, but knowing, somehow, that there was more. And suddenly, there's this suave – in her eyes – New Yorker. Willing to take her away from all that, willing to make it legal . . .

'It must have been pretty enticing,' I said thoughtfully.

Allison laughed, a sorry little sound. 'It's hard to remember,' she admitted. 'I was as naive as . . . Seymour!'

'No-one was ever as naive as Seymour,' I assured her with a smile.

'I was,' she insisted softly, her eyes cloudy and far away.

'But Phil was . . . good to you.' I said it tentatively.

'Oh, yes,' Allison shrugged. 'He was good to me.' She looked at me quizzically. 'But . . . you knew that.'

Wrong. *Nick* knew that. And Nick had not fallen into bed with his partner's wife, possibly because he knew that Phil loved Allison.

'Phil loved you,' I said.

'I don't understand, Nick,' Allison frowned. 'Why are you doing this *now*?'

I shrugged helplessly. 'I don't know, I guess I'm just trying to . . . sort things out.' It was a feeble sounding explanation, but it was something.

'It doesn't matter, now,' Allison said firmly. 'I didn't love him.' She looked up at me, her green eyes limpid and candid. 'I think the only man I've ever loved is you.'

'Oh, boy,' I said softly.

When she curled around and stood up on her tiptoes to kiss me, I made no move to stop her. When she threw her arms around my neck and pulled me closer, I made no move to stop her. And when we finally broke apart, I saw that her eyes were as glazed over with passion as mine must have been. The scent of gardenias permeated the air, made me dizzy . . .

I forgot where I was – on a busy street in Manhattan, with an unnamed danger and crowds of people surging around us. And I certainly forgot *who* I was supposed to be: kissing Allison Grimsley had that kind of effect on me. We were tucked back into a shadowy alcove, and I had the feeling that we might just melt together into the pavement if this continued . . .

'Nick!' Allison broke away, breathlessly.

'Hmm . . .' I nuzzled her neck.

'Where's that cab?' Her words were soft and breathless in my ear.

'Good idea,' I said. I looked up the street to the corner. I could see traffic continuing to slide up and down the avenue; I saw a couple of cabs whiz by; but Seymour was nowhere to be seen.

'Damn,' I muttered, pulling up the collar of my tuxedo. 'I'll go find one.'

'Hurry,' Allison said in a throaty growl, and my knees went weak for a moment.

I glanced up as I ducked out from under the protective awning. Right at that moment, there was another flash of lightning, followed by an immediate clap of thunder. Huge, fat drops splattered then thickened and the beginnings of a heavy downpour were on us.

'Perfect,' I muttered to myself, trotting briskly through the rain.

What the hell had happened to Seymour? And where the hell was a cab? And did Nick Allen have any condoms in his nightstand? I headed for Madison, asking myself all the important questions.

I was only a few yards away from the club when I heard a whining sound pass my ear, and then a distinctive ping! as the bullet – intended for my head – ricocheted off the nearby granite wall.

'Holy . . .' I said, ducking instinctively into the closest

doorway. My heart was going triple time as I flattened myself against the rough granite, willing myself to be invisible in the midst of the downpour.

Ping! Another shot whizzed by me, uncomfortably close.

'Nick!' I heard Allison's voice, high pitched with fear. 'Nick!'

'Stay where you are!' I yelled, frightened that she'd come after me and expose herself to the gunman.

'Nick!' her frightened shout came again. 'Watch out! Someone's shooting!'

Ping!

'Are you all right?' Allison's voice was filled with panic.

'Don't move!' I yelled. Oh, God, I thought, make her listen to me! What if somebody tries to snatch her, what if somebody tries to harm her . . . I had to get to her!

I made a sudden move to break away from my shelter, and as I did, through the sheeting gray rain, I saw the flash of a pistol.

'Jesus!' I jumped back relexively, hugging the wall as the bullet hit right next to my face. Its impact sent splintering slivers off the stone.

The gunman was good. Too good.

But I couldn't just stay there. Cursing myself for having been stupid enough to think I could get through this without carrying Nick's gun, I ducked low to the ground and made a dash through the heavy rain.

Those few yards back to the club were the longest yards of my life. I was certain every blundering step of the way that another bullet, this one with Nick's name on it, would find its mark.

But somehow, I made it, panting and frightened, to the shelter of the awning, and dove into the alcove beside Allison, who was huddled on the ground. She had gone white and shaky with the sounds of the gunfire, but I was glad her knees had buckled – it had kept her out of the line of fire.

'Are you all right?' I grabbed her by the arms. 'Allison!'

'Oh, my God!' she gasped, looking at me with eyes gone huge with fear. 'Nick!'

She was terrified, but she wasn't hurt. I breathed a sigh of relief.

'It's OK,' I assured her. 'It's OK.'

Allison glanced wildly around. 'Where . . . where is he?' she whispered. She was trembling.

'The alley.' I gestured towards the ominous, dark passageway yawning halfway down the block, the place the shots had come from. 'At least, he was.'

I caught my breath, then cautiously eased my face around the corner to look. But there was no-one to be seen. The storm had emptied the street of most of its foot traffic, and there was only rain, and more rain, splattering down on the lamplit pavement.

I stood up slowly, then reached down to help Allison to her feet.

'He's gone,' I assured her. 'We're OK.'

'For now . . .' Allison whispered. 'Oh, Nick, who's trying to kill us?'

I believed her fright was genuine.

'I don't know,' I said gently, 'but I'm going to find out.'

Her green eyes went even wider as she stared up at my face. 'You're bleeding,' she said.

She touched my face with a cautious hand, then pulled it away to show me a smear of blood on the tip of her index finger.

I looked at my reflection in the glass of a small window by the club door, and saw Bogie's worn face creased with yet another distinguishing character mark. It wasn't serious, just a grazing little cut where a chip of stone had hit it.

'It's just a scratch,' I assured Allison, and then I couldn't resist adding, 'Angel.' With that lip-curling sneer.

'I think you should go to the hospital,' Allison said seriously.

'I think I should go get my gun,' I said, shaking my head.

Allison sighed, a shuddery, frightened sound which whispered in the night, just the way the rain did.

'So much . . . violence,' she said softly.

Just then, a checkered cab slid up to the end of the awning. The rear door opened, and Seymour peered out, breathless and eager.

'Sorry it took so long,' he panted.

CHAPTER SEVENTEEN

I pushed Allison hurriedly in front of me into the waiting cab, and tumbled in after her, slamming the door behind us. I breathed a sigh of relief. We seemed, for the moment at least, to be safe; but there was no sense in exposing ourselves to any lurking danger any longer than necessary. And glass windows could easily be shattered with a bullet.

'Gotham Towers,' I told the cabbie, and the cab slid quickly away from the curb on slick streets. 'And step on it.'

'Nick!' Seymour exclaimed, 'you're creased!' He was staring at my face with an expression of awe, delight and horror all mixed up together on his. 'There's . . . blood on your cheek!'

'Someone shot at us,' Allison told him.

I pulled a square of silk from my tux pocket and dabbed at the scrape.

'Klapper!' Seymour breathed. 'Nick, it was Klapper! It had to be!'

'Maybe,' I said, studying the silk square. The blood made a neat little splatter pattern on the silk. I looked up at Seymour. 'What took you so long?' I asked him bluntly.

Seymour rolled his eyes behind those thick lenses. 'The canaries were harder to find than a hooker on a Sunday morning!' he explained eagerly.

'The canar . . .' I sighed. Here we went again with that nonsense tough guy talk. 'There were plenty of cabs, from what I could see.'

'I had to hoof it down to Madison,' Seymour said, 'and everyone was scrambling like crazy to get out of the sizzle. When I finally managed to flag this one down, some other hard Harry with a kisser that could break a mirror in the next apartment stepped on my daisy crushers and tried to . . .'

'Stop it!' I shouted.

Seymour jumped. Beside me, I felt Allison start with surprise, too.

'But Nick . . .' Seymour began. 'I was just trying to tell you . . .'

I cut him off with an angry gesture. 'Just stop it, Seymour!' I stared coldly at him. 'Let's get real, here, OK? You think you can manage that for a minute?'

Seymour stared blankly at me. 'What are you talking about?' he asked meekly.

'What I'm talking about is . . . talking!' Now *there* was a pithy explanation!

'Huh?'

'Your words,' I said through clenched teeth. 'Listen to how you sound. It's unreal! No-one could possibly *really* be as nerdy as you!'

Allison and Seymour exchanged puzzled glances. 'Nerdy?' they chorused.

Oh, Christ. What was the early fifties equivalent of that word?

'Wimpy!' I said.

They still looked puzzled.

'Wussy! Dopey . . .' I wracked my brain for the correct simile. 'Goofy!' I shouted.

That one seemed to do the trick. Seymour's immature face flushed with sudden realization and hurt. His eyes actually began to tear.

'You . . . you don't mean that, Nick,' he said tentatively.

I could see he didn't want to believe what he was hearing from his ultimate hero.

But I didn't care. I was fed up with his ridiculous, maze-like patter and his feeble attempt at tough-guy attitude. The kid couldn't even flag down a cab in time to keep me from a bullet, for Christ's sake!

'I meant every word of it,' I told him flatly. 'You've been sticking closer to me than my underwear, and it's getting boring.'

Allison put a restraining hand on my arm. 'Take it easy, Nick,' she said softly. 'He's just a kid, and he's only trying to help . . .'

I glanced at her, then looked back at Seymour, who seemed to be shrinking into the corner of the seat. 'Well, he's not helping!' I spat. 'And it's about time he learned that he's never going to be a Sam Spade or a Philip Marlowe or a Thomas Magnum. So he might as well stop trying to sound like them!'

'Magnum?' Allison echoed, puzzled.

'Never mind,' I said hastily.

Seymour looked at me with beseeching eyes, the eyes of a wounded spaniel. 'But . . . I don't want to be like any of those guys,' he said earnestly. 'I just want to be like you.'

'Me?' I laughed cynically.

'I can learn . . .' Seymour began eagerly.

'Kid,' I broke off his speech with a flat handed gesture. 'Listen, you *don't* want to be like me. If I'm real lucky, I might get to spend the rest of my life leaping from one place to another . . . instead of lying face down in a pool of blood.'

Beside me, Allison shivered, even though she couldn't have had any idea what I meant by 'leaping.' It was the reference to blood.

'I don't understand,' Seymour said tentatively.

163

'There's nothing to understand,' I told him coldly. 'That's not your job.' I glanced at the front of the cab. 'Cabbie . . . pull over!'

'I was!' the cabbie said indignantly, squealing to a stop on a rain slicked street.

Then I realized that we had arrived in front of our intended destination, the Gotham. Where the gun, possibly my key to my future, lay locked away.

I looked flatly into Seymour's eyes. I steeled myself against his pleading look. 'It's done, Seymour,' I told him. 'Over. And out.' I opened the door and pointed towards the street.

'Nick . . .' Allison said pleadingly.

I shook my head. 'From now on,' I said to Seymour, 'you find some other sucker of a shamus to pester. I don't have the time.'

'Nick, you're tired and you're hurt,' Allison said.

'I'm fine,' I said through clenched teeth.

She looked over at Seymour, who seemed utterly devastated by my words. 'He doesn't mean it,' she said soothingly.

Seymour looked at me through teary eyes. 'I think he does,' he said.

'Yes,' I confirmed, 'I do.'

After one last sad look at me, he climbed slowly out of the cab, bent like an old man. I saw him disappear into the rain.

Allison turned angrily towards me. 'You didn't have to do that to him!' she exclaimed. 'That was . . . just plain mean!'

'Sometimes, Angel,' I said with a sneer, 'mean is the best medicine there is.' I felt like an utter heel, but I had done what I had to do.

I scrambled out of the cab. Allison began to follow me, but I shook my head no. Who knew what lurked in the dark halls of the Gotham Towers? She was safer waiting in the cab. It was dark and anonymous, and a good distance from the hidden recesses of the darkened building.

'Just wait here,' I told her. 'I'll be back in a minute.'

Before she could protest – and the skirts always do protest – I was out of the cab and dashing through the rain, into the darkened building. I jogged rapidly through the empty, silent lobby and pressed the button for the elevator, praying for a quick arrival. I felt exposed here.

The elevator seemed to take for ever to arrive. I got in, first checking to make sure the car was really there. I rode safely up to the fifth floor.

I got out there, then hightailed it rapidly to the stairs and climbed down – an evasive measure I'd seen on countless detective series. Making as little noise as possible, I pushed open the fire door that led to the fourth floor, and crept cautiously down the hallway towards the office.

I wasn't taking any chances: my ears and eyes were alert for anything that might signal an intruder, someone waiting to do me harm.

But it was silent, dead silent, on the fourth floor. And I reached the office without incident. Inside, I was just as careful: lockpicks were easy to come by and, in the right hands, even easier to use. And I had a feeling that breaking and entering might be among the evasive Klapper's many talents. But a quick look around convinced me that it, too, was empty and safe. For the moment.

I hurried quietly across the room and snapped on a little goosenecked desk lamp – no sense in drawing attention to my presence. Then I took the snubnosed .38 from the desk drawer where I'd left it. I hefted the piece in my hand, feeling the ominous weight of it, staring at the cold glint it gave off in the dim yellow light.

I hesitated for a moment: did I really want to do this? But then I realized, it wasn't for me. It was for Nick Allen. And Allison. Whatever Sam Beckett's objections to this kind of defense might be, they had no place here, not in this dark world where shadowy pursuers lurked, armed and waiting, ready to kill.

I nodded, my mind made up. Then I shrugged into the leather harness and fit the gun snugly to my side. Grimacing, I pulled on Phil's ill-fitting hat and trench-coat – I'd left Nick's at his apartment, and I wanted some sort of protection from the rain.

I stared at my battered reflection in the cracked dim mirror above the dusty filing cabinet. 'Time to go, tough guy,' I told the reflection. 'Time to catch the bad guy.' Then I flicked off the light and left, pulling the door shut and locked behind me.

I walked cautiously down the darkened hallway again, went up the stairs one flight, and found the elevator still open, waiting for me. That was a good sign. It meant I hadn't been tailed – not unless the killer was waiting for me in the lobby. I punched the lobby button and rode down. When the doors opened, I saw a movement out of the corner of my eye, and tensed, reaching for my gun.

But then I realized it was only Seymour, and without really looking, I could see that he was fumbling for a box of tissues at his concession stand.

No, I told myself, be firm.

I started resolutely across the lobby, my heels making a clicking sound on the marble floor. Then I heard a noise behind me, and I froze in my tracks. I knew that noise. It was the sound of Seymour's glasses hitting the floor. And I knew without looking that the right lens would pop out again, like it had this morning. And that he would be fumbling blindly around . . . damn it, I told myself, don't go getting soft, not now.

'Darn . . .' I heard him mutter.

I sighed, I paused.

'Darn,' I heard again.

I gave up, and turned around.

Sure enough, there was Seymour, down on his knees in a repeat performance of earlier that day, groping for the lens. I closed my eyes for a beat. When I opened them, the scene was still the same.

I shook my head and walked over to Seymour. He didn't look up. I took the glasses from him and popped the lens easily back into place.

'Thank you.' Seymour's voice was low, his eyes remained focussed on the floor.

'Seymour,' I said, 'look at me.'

He looked up. 'What is it?' he asked defensively, his eyes wide and wounded behind those magnified, coke bottle lenses.

'I've hurt one friend already tonight,' I told him. 'I don't want to make it a practice.'

He just stared at me, puzzled.

'Seymour,' I said, 'I'm trying to tell you I'm sorry. You're not a nerd. Or a wuss or a wimp . . . or any of the other names I called you before.'

'It's OK,' Seymour muttered.

Jeeze, I thought, I've done permanent damage to his psyche!

'No,' I said firmly, 'it's not OK, because it's not true. The truth is that you're really a neat kid . . . and a really good friend. You're exactly the kind of person a guy can always count on, and that's the reason I said what I did.'

'I still don't get it,' Seymour said, confused.

I looked him straight in the eye, man to man. 'I'm going after the Klapper,' I told him confidentially. 'He's a very dangerous man – more dangerous than even I imagined. And I didn't want you tagging along.'

'Oh!' Realization dawned behind Seymour's glasses. 'You mean . . . you were afraid I'd get hurt?'

'Well, yeah,' I said.

'Gee, Nick,' Seymour said.

'Or get in the way.' After all, I didn't want him to get *too* cocky. 'So,' I said, clapping my hands together briskly, 'now that that's all straightened out, I'll see you later.'

'Later?' Seymour asked. 'What do you mean?'

'I've got to get going.'

I turned and headed briskly for the doors, but it wasn't going to be that easy, not by a long shot. Seymour tagged after me like an eager puppy.

'Who is he, Nick?' he asked eagerly. 'Do you know yet?'

I shook my head. 'No. I still don't know,' I told him. 'For a while, I thought he might be . . . you.'

'Me!' Seymour's expression went from shock to delight at even being *considered* for the role of dangerous criminal, then back to shock. 'Why?'

'Well,' I ticked the reasons off on my fingers, 'First, you practically pushed me into the elevator when there *was* no elevator. And second, earlier tonight, when the Klapper . . . tried to fog me, you were flagging a canary!' I smiled at him as I used his vernacular.

Seymour pondered this information for a moment. 'Gosh,' he said finally, 'it really could have been me!' I could tell he was flattered. Then he added quickly, 'But it wasn't, Nick! Honest!'

I nodded seriously. 'I know. I realized it when we were in the cab.'

'What happened in the cab?' Seymour asked, puzzled.

'Well,' I said, 'it was raining when Klapper shot at me

168

from the alley. If you were the Klapper, you would have been soaked.'

'Gosh!' Seymour said again, with admiration in his voice. 'That's real deductive logic.'

'Uh-huh,' I agreed modestly.

'But . . . if you don't know who he is . . .' Seymour let the sentence trail off into an unasked question.

'I know where he is,' I said.

'You do?' His face lit up. 'Then, we're going after him!'

I stopped in my tracks and stared at him. 'No,' I told him firmly. 'We aren't going after him. I'm going after him. Alone. Capishe?'

'Nick, please!' Seymour said earnestly. 'I can help! I can be an extra pair of peepers for you. I can cover your . . . seat.'

'Absolutely not,' I said.

'Nick, after what you said to me before, you owe this to me.' Seymour's eyes were large and sincere . . . and guilt producing.

I looked up heavenward, as if I was going to get any help from that section! Finally, I nodded, giving in. 'OK,' I said.

'Neat!' Seymour exclaimed.

I winced. 'OK, but on two conditions,' I said warningly.

'Name 'em!' Seymour grinned.

'First, you follow my orders to the letter.'

Seymour nodded. 'What else?' he asked eagerly.

'You get a raincoat so you don't catch pneumonia,' I said.

At first, Seymour looked as if he was going to balk. But he took in my no-nonsense expression, and nodded. 'Gotcha!' he said.

I bit back a smile as he turned and raced clumsily for the newsstand. I watched as he fumbled around behind it, and came up with the most pitiful, crumpled looking thing I had ever seen, outside of a Columbo episode, that is. As he turned to try to untangle it and get himself into it, I promptly headed through the doors.

'Goodbye, Seymour,' I said in a whisper.

I dashed out into the night and headed for the cab. Then I stopped short. The cab was pulling rapidly away from the curb.

I watched, completely bewildered, as it rolled down the street and away from me. Then, there was no cab. That is, all I could see were red taillights, dim and blurred in the sheeting rain, as the cab sped away, carrying Allison with it.

I stood there, stunned. This just didn't make any sense. But it had happened. The streets, late at night and soaked, glistened with rainbows of oil and broken dreams.

'Allison,' I whispered.

Where was she going? And who was she? I mean, *really*, who was she?

Just then, I heard a panting and snuffling sound, and Seymour appeared beside me, still struggling into the crumpled, oversized raincoat.

He didn't seem to understand that I had left him behind on purpose. He followed my distant gaze down the rainslicked street.

'Just missed a cab, huh?' he said.

I sighed.

A moment later, he asked, puzzled, 'Where's Allison?'

'That's the sixty four thousand dollar question, Seymour,' I said grimly.

There were two choices. One was that Al had been right – that Allison was behind all the evil events that had occurred, and was even now, winging her way to parts unknown. Or Rio.

The other was that someone – presumably the Klapper

– had snatched her for his own nefarious purposes. Although I liked the second theory better, I knew damned well that Allison's chances of survival would be much greater if she proved to be the villainess.

One way or another, I had to find her to wrap this case up. At least, that was what it looked like to me. I turned to Seymour, just two lonely trenchcoated guys, standing in the rain.

'We've got to find her,' I told him.

'Is it a matter of life and death?' he asked eagerly.

I nodded grimly. I wasn't sure whose life and death: it might be just Nick Allen's, it might be Allison's and Seymour's, as well.

'Yes,' I said. 'That's exactly what it is.'

CHAPTER EIGHTEEN

'Great!' said Seymour enthusiastically. 'Let's go!'

This was no time to quibble about him accompanying me. Maybe an extra pair of eyes and ears really would help.

'OK,' I said, resigned.

I flagged down the first passing cab I saw, and we scrambled hurriedly in. A plan was forming in my mind as we swept along the wet city streets, but first, I had to check out some information. Seymour, sitting beside me, seemed to sense my preoccupation enough to not ask any questions – although I could almost feel his curiosity bursting out of him.

Back on 58th, I told the cabbie to stop. I flew into the Blue Island again, and spent a fast five minutes bribing and shaking questions out of the staff there. I thought the clue to who and where Klapper was would lie with someone in the club, and I didn't care what it cost me to get the information out of people.

Fortunately, with my Bogey visage and snarling attitude, money sufficed, and I didn't have to resort to violence. Unfortunately, I was convinced fairly quickly that no-one there knew anything, although they all seemed extremely willing to try to help. Or at least, to take my money.

Frustrated, I ran from the club. As I slammed the cab door behind me again, I leaned forward. 'LaGuardia!' I told the driver. 'As fast as you can – I'll make it worth your while!'

'Gotcha, bud!' the driver replied, and squealed away from the curb.

Seymour couldn't restrain himself any longer. 'Come on, Nick!'

'What is it, kid?' I said, distracted.

'I got it!' he said excitedly. 'This has got to be it. Tell me if I'm right — you laid a Ben Franklin on the cocktail shaker at the gin joint, and he opened up like a Toledo pencil pusher on his third martini and sang like Tweety Bird.' He looked expectantly at me. 'That's it, isn't it?'

I thought about it for a moment, then began to translate, thinking as I went. 'I gave a . . . hundred dollars to the . . . bartender at the Blue Lagoon. And . . . he talked as much as an accountant from Toledo on vacation who's had one too many?'

'Well, of course. That's what I just said,' Seymour said, puzzled.

'Oh my God,' I said softly, 'I understood you.' It was a horrific concept.

'Am I right?' Seymour persisted.

'No,' I replied, shaking my head. 'You're wrong.'

Seymour sagged back against the cracked leather seat of the cab, obviously disappointed. 'Then how do you know Klapper's taking Allison to LaGuardia?' he asked plaintively.

'And not vice versa?' Al materialized unexpectedly on the jump seat across from us. 'The kid's got a point, Sam. Are you certain it isn't the other way around — Allison taking Klapper to LaGuardia?'

I didn't even mind that he was sticking to his same old suspicions; I was never so glad to see anyone in my life. 'Al!' I exclaimed.

'Al told you?' Seymour said, completely confused. 'Who's Al?'

I stared at Al who stared right back with a kind of calm, quizzical look. It was clear to me that this was the time to make up for some of the damage I'd caused before. Mend some fences.

'He's a friend,' I told Seymour, looking at Al while I said it. 'A very good friend.'

'Oh, yeah?' Seymour said.

'Maybe the best friend I've ever had.'

Al snorted. 'Let's not get carried away, Sam,' he cautioned me. 'Guilt is one thing – it certainly has its uses in life – but there's no need to get into mushy hyperbole, it's embarrassing.'

Seymour, oblivious to this exchange, pressed on. 'So this guy Al is your source?'

'Uh huh,' I said, 'you could call him that.'

'Then he's the one who tipped you to the Klapper?'

'He tried to,' I said, still looking at Al. 'He tried to tip me to a lot of things, but I wouldn't listen. I got all bent out of shape.'

Al had the grace to shrug modestly. 'Well . . . maybe I did go a bit too far.' He shrugged again. 'But you know, that kind of thing just happens, sometimes. Even between friends.'

'You got . . . bent out of shape?' Seymour echoed, puzzled. 'What's that?'

Language gap again. 'I got angry,' I explained. 'And I got carried away, said some things I shouldn't have said. Things I regret.'

'Oh.' Seymour's face lit up with understanding. 'Now I get it – it's what you were talking about before. He's the *other* friend you hurt tonight?'

I winced. 'I'm afraid so,' I said humbly.

'Sam . . .' Al shook his head in reproach, but I had more than a sneaking suspicion that he was pleased at what he had just heard.

'And I'll bet you didn't want to hurt him, either, did you, Nick?'

'Seymour . . .' I said pleadingly. Nothing like having your guts exposed.

'Hurt?' Al grinned triumphantly at me.

'Ah . . .' Talk about feeling like a jerk! The two of them in one cab – even though Seymour didn't know there *were* two of them there – it was enough to make me cringe for my earlier behavior. Still, I reasoned with myself, enough was enough – a man could only apologize so many times, then he had to let it go. Besides, I hadn't done anything *that* terrible.

Al seemed to sense my change in outlook. He looked around curiously, then rubbed his hands together. 'So,' he said, 'where are we going, Sam?'

'LaGuardia,' I said.

'I heard you the first time, bud,' the cab driver piped up from the front seat.

'I don't think this is such a good idea,' Al said cautiously.

'I don't care,' I said calmly.

The cabbie twisted around in his seat. 'What's the matter with you?' he snarled. 'Don't you got no manners . . .' His eyes widened. 'Oh! Mr Bogart, I'm sorry.'

'Ah . . . no, please, don't apologize,' I said hastily. 'I'm just . . . distracted.'

'Can I have your autograph?' the cabbie asked, shoving a Dodgers' programme in the back seat.

I sighed. 'Sure,' I said. Why not. I signed 'Humphrey Bogart' with a flourish and handed it back to him.

'Gee, thanks!' said the cabbie.

We rode in silence the rest of the way, although Al was chuckling to himself, and Seymour did throw a few guarded glances in my direction. I felt like telling *him* to try holding a conversation with someone who was visible only to him, but what was the point?

The trip seemed endless. I couldn't stop thinking about Allison – whether or not she was all right, whether or not she was . . . involved. Finally, the checkered cab pulled to the curb at LaGuardia.

I hastily paid the cabbie and got out of the cab, glancing cautiously around me. Seymour stood beside me, looking a little intimidated. Al, of course, didn't bother with traditional exits: he stood up right through the roof of the cab.

'I'm telling you, this is very dangerous, Sam,' he warned me.

The cab sped away right through him, and he sauntered over to join us at the curb.

'Allison is here somewhere,' I reminded him.

'And that's precisely why it's so dangerous,' he retorted.

Seymour thought I was talking to him.

'I'll be careful, Nick, I promise!' he said.

'OK, OK,' I muttered.

Seymour looked up and down the length of the building. 'This is a big bird roost,' he said, nodding. 'But between the two of us, we'll find her, don't worry.'

'I know,' I agreed. I jerked my thumb toward one end of the building. 'You start at that side. I'll start from this one – we'll meet up in the middle.'

Seymour nodded seriously. 'Gotcha,' he said.

'Notice everything,' I said to him. 'Any little thing might be important.'

'I will,' he said solemnly. 'I know.'

He turned and began to walk away, but I grabbed him by the sleeve of his raincoat. 'Seymour,' I said reluctantly, 'there's something you have to know for your own protection.'

'What?' he asked.

I sighed. 'It's . . . well, it's just *possible* that Allison may have hired the Klapper to kill Phil.' There, it was out.

'Thank you for not letting him walk into this blind,' Al said to me.

Seymour looked shocked. 'Nick, you can't believe that!'

'No,' I said, 'I don't.'

'Aw, for Christ's sake, Sam,' Al shook his head in disgust.

'But as long as it's even a slight possibility,' I continued, 'if you . . . uh . . . eyeball my main squeeze, I want you to Peeping Tom her completely on the q.t. until you can semaphore me.'

'Your main squeeze?' Seymour's brow wrinkled in confusion.

'Allison,' I explained.

He seemed to mull it over. 'Main squeeze,' he repeated. 'Huh. I like it – I gotta remember that one.' He nodded decisively. 'OK, Nick, I'm shaggin'.' And he was off.

I turned to face Al who looked almost as puzzled as Seymour had. 'What's the matter, Al?' I grinned at him. 'It's the shamus talking. I thought you were up on this private eye lingo.'

'Oh, I understood you, all right,' Al said. 'I'm just trying to figure out how the phrase "main squeeze" is going to get from Seymour's vocabulary to black slang in the next twenty years.'

I was startled for a moment, then I laughed. But the laughter didn't last long. 'Come on,' I said to Al. 'We're here for a reason.'

'Yes,' he said cynically, 'and the reason has Swiss watch hip movement.'

Inside the LaGuardia terminal, at this time of night,

it was virtually empty. These were the days before round the clock flights, instant business meetings and the driving hurry to be somewhere the day before yesterday. Most of the counters were closed down till the morning. An elderly black man swabbed down the floor near the middle of the concourse, while no more than two dozen weary looking people waited for a morning flight, clutching luggage, briefcases and early edition newspapers.

I had pulled off Phil's trenchcoat and fedora on our way into the terminal, and as we strode through the place, I held the coat slung casually over one arm as I surveyed my surroundings.

Al glanced at it. 'I assume you've got a roscoe under that fedora,' he remarked.

'Yup,' I confirmed his suspicion in my best terse Gary Cooper imitation.

'Uh huh,' Al nodded sagely. 'That's good. Could you use it?'

'Yup.' I kept walking.

'Uh huh.' Al nodded again. 'Could you use it on Allison if you had to?'

I thought about it for a moment. 'Probably not,' I said honestly.

'Oh, great!' Al threw his hands up in the air. 'That's it!' He peeled abruptly away and headed off in another direction.

'Where are you going?' I said.

'To check the Ladies Room,' Al replied matter of factly.

'Al!' I said, shocked.

He threw me a 'give me a break' look. 'Somebody has to do it,' he said condescendingly. 'Allison is a woman. And I certainly wouldn't advise you going in there!'

He had a point. I shrugged and nodded, then watched him as he moved off. I kept on going, checking out everyone and everything. Far down at the other end of the terminal, I could see Seymour walking deliberately through the few gathered people, checking things out too. We were wending our way towards one another.

I passed by a couple of very young sailors, asleep in the uncomfortable molded plastic chairs, their duffel bags resting on the floor beside them. No danger there. My eyes swept the rest of the small crowd ahead of me. Then something caught my eye, and I looked again, this time more carefully. There was a man in a raincoat and a slouch hat at the ticket counter. Hmm, I thought . . .

I slowed down and stared, my suspicions aroused by the hidden looks, the furtive posture of the man at the ticket counter. I tried to signal Seymour without really drawing attention to myself, but he was preoccupied in his own search, and he didn't even notice.

Suddenly, there was a distraction, a commotion among the waiting passengers.

'Bogie!'

I turned and saw a funny looking kid with red hair and black rimmed glasses, pointing at me.

'Bogie!

I stiffened.

'Don't point, Allen!' His mother grabbed his arm and forced it down. 'It's not polite!'

'But mom,' the kid whined, 'look! It's Humphrey Bogart!'

Oh, no, I thought, as the kid eluded his mother's grasp and darted between the waiting passengers, heading determinedly in my direction. This is all I need, I thought. Oh no, oh no, oh no!

'Mister Bogart!' he shouted.

Oh yes.

So much for keeping a low profile, I thought. I saw the man at the counter glance quickly up at me, then just as quickly look away. He looked familiar, but it was such a fleeting glimpse that I couldn't identify him.

Then the kid was in front of me, harried mother in hot pursuit. A few of the other passengers were now staring in my direction, as well, nudging each other and exchanging murmured remarks.

'It *is* you!' the kid shouted, delighted. 'Oh, boy! I knew it!'

I looked down at him. Now this, I thought, is weird. How could an eight-ish year old kid in 1953 look so familiar to me? But he did. There was something about him . . .

The kid was hopping up and down with excitement. 'Mom!'

'Allen! Leave that poor man alone!' His mother, a thin, frazzled matron finally caught up with her son.

'I love your movies!' the kid exclaimed, ignoring his mother. 'I've seen them all!'

Oh my God, I thought, realization dawning . . .

'Ever since I could curl my lip I wanted to be just like you. I practiced so much my mom took me to an analyst!'

It couldn't be . . .

'I even dream you talk to me, you know, that you give me advice!' His eyes were bright behind the glasses. 'Like how to get Annie up to my room . . .'

No. No way . . .

From the corner of my eye, I saw Seymour start in surprise, then approach the furtive man at the ticket counter. I was too far away to make out what they were saying, but they were definitely talking.

'Kid . . .' I said, moving away. I had a feeling I had better get over there, and quick.

'Oh, Mr Bogart, please!' he begged, tugging at my sleeve. 'Just a little advice. My analyst calls it neurotic, this need to fantasize – that's what he calls it – about a hero figure, but . . .'

It was.

I tried to disentangle myself, but the young Woody Allen had a surprisingly strong grip, and he was one determined kid.

'Allen!' his mother screeched ineffectually.

'. . . but if he had to live with my mother, he'd be neurotic too!'

I could see that Seymour had sort of frozen in place, an unnaturally quiet pose.

'She drives me bananas!'

And then Seymour began to move, move with the stiff unyielding posture of a man walking against his will. Like someone forced to move. Like someone with a . . . gun in his ribs.

'Jesus!' I exclaimed, and broke away from the kid as his mother grabbed him by the ear and pulled hard, throwing him mercifully off balance.

'See what you did? You created a scene!' I could hear her yelling as I ran.

'I just wanted his autograph,' wailed Woody.

'You embarrassed him!'

I broke through the crowd and raced towards the spot where the man was hustling Seymour around the corner and towards the exit.

'Seymour!' I shouted.

I saw him throw a look of complete panic in my direction, and then he was yanked through the doors and into the foggy night.

CHAPTER NINETEEN

I barreled through the terminal and slammed out the doors Seymour and his captor had disappeared through, then came to a surprised halt. I found myself suddenly on a dark, fog-swept tarmac.

It was an eerie place, full of shadows and dim forms. As my eyes adjusted to the misty darkness, I could just make out the dark shapes of a fuel truck, and an idling DC-3 with a loading staircase up against its side. There were a few baggage carts resting nearby. But there wasn't a single person to be seen.

Then something moved, something that had been standing still in the shadow of the landing gear. As I peered through the fog, I could see Seymour, still being hustled along against his will. Then I caught a glimpse of the man in the raincoat.

'Lionel!' I shouted, shocked, as the truth finally dawned on me. 'Let him go!'

But Lionel didn't answer. Instead, using Seymour as a shield, the Gotham Building Superintendent ran across the tarmac, shooting in my direction as he went.

The sound was loud and startling in the dense night. I just managed to dive behind one of the luggage carts in time, as the bullets from the big .45 he carried plowed into the stacked baggage. Suitcases shattered under the impact, and clothing spilled on to the concrete.

'Jesus,' I whispered to myself. Lionel.

Without giving myself time to think about it, I yanked the .38 into firing position and sprinted across the tarmac.

I saw Lionel force Seymour into the black abyss of the hangar.

I moved silently up to the hangar door and peered cautiously around the corner. Nothing. No people, no movement. I knew I had to just act, had to get in there and save Seymour. I couldn't even let myself linger on the discovery I had just made – the fact that the killer, Klapper, had proved to be someone I wouldn't have suspected in a million years. Mild mannered Lionel, I thought ruefully. Some detective I was.

But there was no time. Not now. Moving stealthily, I slipped into the dark hangar and ducked behind a Staggerwing Beech. I squinted, trying to spot Lionel among the dark forms of the large, shadowy aircraft. Then I couldn't see them at all.

I heard a shout. 'Nick!' It was Lionel's voice, and it came from the vicinity of a Lockheed Electra which stood in the corner of the hangar.

'Lionel!' I yelled back, 'let him go!'

'We don't want to hurt him!' Lionel's voice was strained and nervous.

We? 'What *do* you want?' I shouted.

'All Allison and I want is to get out of New York!'

We! Allison! No, I thought, there was no way I could believe that Allison could ever have had anything to do with Lionel. But just hearing her name sent a chill down my spine.

'Where is she, Lionel?' I shouted. 'Tell me where she is!' I tried to keep the panic out of my voice.

I ventured to peer around the large radial engine of the Staggerwing, and then had to throw myself to the ground as a bullet sparked off the cylinder head, just inches away from me.

'Nick, you have to face reality!' Lionel's voice was hoarse, strained.

Hah! I thought. Reality – that was good, considering the source. But I remembered something about hostage negotiation – the longer you can keep the captor talking, the better chance you have . . .

'What reality, Lionel?' I yelled.

'She doesn't love you!' he shouted. 'She doesn't love you any more than she loved Phil!'

So it had all been Lionel. All along! 'Is that why you killed him?' I said bluntly.

'He wouldn't face the truth!' Lionel screamed.

Oh, Jesus, I thought, have I set him off?

'What truth is that?' I played for time.

'Love! That's what it's all about Nick!' I could tell now his voice was coming from the hatch of the aircraft. If I could just get over there . . .

'Love,' I echoed incredulously.

'Phil couldn't take it, Nick. We had no other choice.'

I still was unnerved by his use of the word 'we.' 'You've always got a choice, Lionel!' I screamed.

'No,' he insisted. 'But you've got one now – you're smart, Nick, a lot smarter than Phil was. Grab your chance and get out of here while you're still able to!'

'Where's Seymour?' I yelled.

'He's right here, with me.' Lionel's voice went up a decibel. 'I'm choking him, Nick.'

I could hear some desperate scrabbling sounds.

'I'm choking him right now. I have to . . . he's gonna have to die, Nick . . .'

And I knew I couldn't wait any longer, I couldn't try to negotiate my way out of this mess. Lionel was obviously over the edge, capable of doing anything to anyone.

There was no time for subtlety or sneaking. I broke from under the wind and threw myself toward the back of the hangar, as Lionel's .45 boomed twice, the slugs tearing right through the plane. I went down in a dive and rolled under the tail as the echoes of the shots reverberated in the hangar.

'How many shots is that?'

Al's voice nearly made me jump out of my skin. 'Jesus!' I gasped. I looked up and saw him standing up beside me. 'Al! Get down!' I hissed.

Al waved my words off. 'Sam, he can't see me or hear me, remember?'

I nodded weakly.

'And he certainly can't shoot me! Sit tight,' Al said. 'I'll find him for you.'

And he was off, strutting across the darkened hangar and up into the Electra with the confidence of a man who knows he's both invisible and invincible.

A moment later, I heard him shout. 'He's right over here, Sam!'

I moved cautiously forward in the direction of Al's voice. I could make out Lionel hovering in the hatch, a limp body at his feet. Oh, God, I thought, Seymour? Allison?

'You bastard!' I screamed, forgetting to be cautious. 'You'll never get away with this . . .'

'Sam!' Al shouted. 'Watch out!'

It *was* a stupid thing to do, giving in to my emotions. Because it let Lionel know exactly where I was. And he fired. I winced as I saw the little trail of flame go right through Al's head!

It didn't bother Al in the least. He just grinned cockily and said, 'You missed!'

Not that Lionel could see or hear him, but it seemed to give Al a perverse pleasure anyway.

'Sam!' I heard Al yell. 'Move to the right a little . . . he doesn't know where you are . . .'

I moved.

'Good,' Al said. Then, 'Oh-oh! He's gonna shoot, Sam, get down!'

I crouched as a shot went wide and past the Stagger-wing.

'Get to the back of the hangar and work toward me!' Al yelled.

I obeyed. It was the most peculiar feeling, it was almost as if I was invisible, too; or as if Al was my guardian angel.

'He's . . . shooting!' Al yelled, and as I hit the ground again, I heard two more shots in rapid succession.

I tried to count, to remember how many shots he'd fired. I thought he might be near the end of his ammunition, but I couldn't be certain . . .

And then I was. Because Al told me . . .

'Sam, now!' I heard Al scream excitedly. 'He's reloading, get him now, Sam! Now!'

I didn't give myself a second to hesitate. I just scrambled to my feet and barrelled out of the shadows and through the hangar. I raced across the space and dove up the steps of the Electra.

I leaped up on Lionel, as, panicked and shaky, he fumbled frantically with the clip. But it was too late: I stuck the .38 against his nose.

'Drop it,' I said harshly.

I saw his eyes swivel down to the gun he still held. 'Don't even think it, see?' I snarled.

Al sighed. 'That's Edward G. Robinson, Sam,' he informed me.

But whoever it was, it seemed to do the trick. Lionel, crazy as he was, wasn't crazy enough to risk getting his brains blown out. He dropped the gun and raised his hands in the air.

'Don't shoot me,' he said meekly.

'Don't tempt me,' I shot back angrily.

At our feet, Seymour began to sit groggily up, his hands touching his throat. I could see the angry red welt left there by Lionel's attempt to choke the life out of him.

'Nick,' he said hoarsely.

'Are you all right?' I asked.

Seymour nodded. 'I'm OK,' he whispered, 'but Allison . . .' He nodded towards the back of the plane, and I saw her

Alive, thank God! Staring at me, green eyes terrified above the gag that covered her mouth. Her hands bound.

'If Lionel makes a move, shoot him,' I said to Seymour, and tossed the gun to him.

Seymour scrambled to his feet and stared grimly at his would be killer. 'No problem,' he assured me.

I made my way quickly through the narrow aisle and released Allison from her bonds. She threw herself into my arms, sobbing.

'Oh, Nick,' she said, 'thank God!'

'It's OK,' I said, 'it's OK.'

'I thought he was going to kill me!'

'You're safe, Angel,' I assured her.

I held her close, and over the top of her head, I could see Al staring at me from the front of the plane. He shook his head with a cynical grin.

'Angel?' he echoed sarcastically. 'Really, Sam, you're gonna have to start thinking up some more original material.'

*   *   *

It was an hour later when all the paper work was finally through, when the uniformed NYPD had arrived, taken our statements, and begun to put the rock-solid case together.

Faced with Nick Allen's gun to his head, the cops, and the undeniable evidence of his own actions, Lionel had unraveled like a cheap suit. His confession was laced through with real insanity – delusions about Allison and her 'true, real' love for him. It was horrible and sad at the same time.

Allison and I leaned wearily against the ticket counter and watched as the cops took Lionel away, handcuffed and babbling to himself.

Beside me, Allison shivered as Lionel cast one last longing look at her. Then he was gone.

'He'll be away for a long, long time,' I told her reassuringly. 'Maybe forever. The last big walk . . .'

Allison hugged me tightly. 'Oh, Nick, I just don't understand.'

'What's to understand?' I asked.

'I don't know – I mean, how could I have turned Lionel on so much and not realized it?'

I shrugged. 'I guess your mind was on other things,' I said.

She sighed. 'You know, the funny part is . . . I feel sorry for him.'

I nodded. 'I know,' I said. 'I guess I do, too. But we can't forget, no matter how sick he is, what he did, Allison.'

'Phil,' she said softly.

I nodded. 'Phil,' I agreed.

Allison shivered again. 'Nick,' she said softly, 'take me away from all this. Please?'

Oh, boy. 'My apartment?' I said.

'I was thinking someplace a little further than that,' Allison said. She held up two airline tickets for me to see.

'Where'd you get those?'

Allison nodded in the direction Lionel and the police had gone. 'I guess some people might think that using these tickets is a little bizarre . . .'

'Yeah,' I said.

'. . . but the poor soul did pay for them.'

There was a pragmatic attitude for you. But coming from Allison who still looked remarkably beautiful, sultry and enticing – despite the evening's wear and tear – it was somehow OK.

'Where are they to?' I asked her.

'Does it matter?' Allison asked.

And right then, staring at her green eyes, shadowed and fatigued, but promising all sorts of wonderful things, I thought no, it doesn't matter in the least.

I reached for her, and kissed her, and the kiss became all-engrossing. Finally, we pulled apart, breathless and starry eyed. No, I thought, it doesn't matter one bit – it could be Timbuktu or Siberia or Rio – as long as she's there . . .

I heard someone clear his throat, and out of the corner of my eye, there was Al, smiling that smart ass smile of him.

'We gotta talk, Sam,' he said.

I sighed. 'You go on ahead on board, Angel,' I told Allison with a perfect lip curl. 'I'll join you in a minute.'

'Don't keep me waiting too long,' Allison said with a throaty purr. 'It's a sleeper flight.'

With that, she took one of the tickets from my hand and walked away. It was a beautiful thing to watch.

Finally I turned to Al. 'What?' I demanded. 'What do you want?'

'I don't think you can get on that plane,' he informed me.

I snorted. 'Oh, I'm getting on that plane, all right,' I said. 'Because if I don't, I'll always regret it. Maybe not today. Maybe not tomorrow. But . . .'

'I saw the picture, Sam,' Al said sarcastically.

'Good. Then you know how it ends.'

'Not with Bogey going off . . .'

'Don't bother me with details,' I said, and turned to follow Allison.

Outside on the foggy tarmac, I strode determinedly towards the DC-3, while Al jogged along beside me.

'Sam,' he said, 'I didn't say you didn't want to go with her. I said, I didn't think you could.'

'And who's going to stop me?' I asked, not breaking stride.

'Nick!' It was Seymour's voice, hoarse and whispery as he came up beside me.

I groaned. 'What?' I said.

'He tried to kill me!' His face was pale and scared, even now. 'Lionel! I thought he was my friend! He tried to choke me to death!'

I took pity on the kid. 'Don't you mean, "the looney tune tried to fog me with a chicken throttle?" ' I joked gently.

'Nick, this was real!' Seymour exclaimed indignantly.

'Well,' I shrugged, 'isn't that what you were looking for, Seymour? A life full of duking it out with Hard Harrys on those long nights as quiet as the city morgue on a slow day?'

Seymour swallowed hard and rubbed his throat. 'Maybe . . . it would be better if I just read about it,' he said dispiritedly.

I stopped and stared at him. This poor kid, someone had to do something to set him straight.

'Maybe you could write about it,' I suggested. I had no idea where the words came from.

To my surprise, Seymour promptly stopped looking depressed, and lit up like a Christmas tree. 'Nick! You mean . . . you read it?'

'What?' I asked, confused. 'Read what?'

'The unfinished manuscript I gave you – *Dead Men Don't Die?* You read it?'

'Oh, my God . . .' I said slowly. 'That . . . you . . .'

'You liked it? You really liked it?' Seymour said eagerly.

'Oh, my God . . .' I said again. '*You're* Rock Roscoe!' Al winked.

'Wow!' Seymour beamed. 'Rock Roscoe? It's *that* tough, huh? Tough enough for a great handle like that . . .' He looked delighted.

'Oh, my God . . .' I repeated.

'It's actually a lot better name than Seymour,' he continued thoughtfully. 'It'll look great on a book jacket.' He beamed. 'Thanks, Nick . . . I'll use it!'

'Nick!' It was Allison's voice.

Seymour and I both looked up. She stood at the foot of the portable stairs leading to the plane, the fog whisping about her.

'Hurry up,' she said. She was a vision.

'Oh, boy,' I whispered. Beside me, Seymour gulped.

Allison turned and climbed the stairs. No-one had ever put as much invitation into a hip movement.

Beside me, Seymour – obviously already slipping into his Rock Roscoe persona – began to describe Allison's ascent in purple prose.

'The fog was as thick as hash house oatmeal and twice as cold, as her hips said goodbye,' he muttered out of the side of his mouth. 'Maybe she was too much moonlight and orchids for the likes of me, but I couldn't help wishing my daisy crushers and hers would be outside the same hotel door . . .' He seemed lost in his own words, and he paused on the tarmac dreamily.

'Get it, Sam?' Al said.

I tried to ignore him. I walked a few steps toward the plane, then turned and stared at him, fuming. 'I can't believe that *this* . . .' I jerked my thumb back to indicate Seymour, who still stood talking tough nonsense on the tarmac, '. . . *this* is why . . .'

Al shrugged. 'That's right,' he said. 'That's why you were sent here. To launch a new novelist . . .'

'A new *pulp* novelist!' I protested.

' . . . pulp novelist who otherwise would have died . . .' Al reminded me.

I looked at Allison disappearing into the plane.

'No . . .' I wailed. 'It's not fair!'

Al shrugged.

I turned and sighed. Behind me, Seymour was frantically scribbling notes on a tattered napkin. The new Mickey Spillane, I thought. And all thanks to me. Rock Roscoe. Oh, boy.

I shook my head and began to walk, wisps of fog rising from the tarmac around my legs.

'You know, Sam,' Al said, walking alongside me, 'I think . . .'

'Don't say it,' I said grimly. 'Don't you dare say it . . .'

'. . . this might be the start of a wonderful friendship.'

'Couldn't resist, could you?' I said glumly.

Al grinned and shrugged.

I looked heavenward.

'OK,' I said grumpily. 'What's next?'

THE END